D1245933

Gullah
Animal Tales

from Daufuskie Island, South Carolina
as told by Albert H. Stoddard

illustrated by Christina Bates
translated & edited by Will Killhour

PUSH BUTTON PUBLISHING COMPANY

Hilton Head Island, South Carolina
1995

PUSH BUTTON PUBLISHING COMPANY
95 Mathews Drive, E/7-131
Hilton Head Island, SC 29926

© 1995, Will Killhour

PUSH BUTTON CORPORATION
7 Hilton Head Terrace
Hilton Head Island, SC 29926

Excerpt from *Orisha: The Gods of Yorubaland* reprinted by permission of Atheneum
Publishers, an imprint of Simon & Schuster

Cataloguing-in-Publication Data

Stoddard, Albert H.
    Gullah animal tales from daufuskie island, south carolina/translated, selected &
    edited by Will Killhour
    1, Folklore of the United States. 2, African American studies. 3, Linguistics -
    African. 4, Southern culture. 5, Mythology -African. 6, Translations of short
    stories - Gullah to English.

1995
ISBN - 0964156679

The basis for the following text came from:

THE LIBRARY OF CONGRESS
Music Division - Recording Laboratory
FOLKLORE OF THE UNITED STATES
Issued from the Folklore Collections
Long-Playing Records L-44, L-45, L-46
ANIMAL TALES TOLD IN THE GULLAH DIALECT
by Albert H. Stoddard of Savannah, GA

CAVEAT PARENTIS

Parents be advised that the folktales contained in this volume have not been paraphrased or corrupted in any way to make them palatable or acceptable to the parents of young children. These stories were not intended to portray the fantasy of a non-violent world; passion, trouble and pain were part of everyday life for most Gullah people. They were not culturally predisposed to keep reality from their children. Thus, I recommend that parents read these stories first before sharing them with younger or more sensitive children.

W.K.

ALBERT H. STODDARD
1872—1954

For all those about to disappear.

ACKNOWLEDGMENTS

During my search for a living correspondent from whom I could learn some of the old stories, people kept steering me towards the wife of a friend of mine, folklorist Carol Roark. Though I couldn't talk her into doing all the research and writing for a volume of Gullah folklore, she did direct me to the Stoddard collection at the Library of Congress.

The people at the Bull Street Library in Savannah, as well as those at the Library of Congress, were helpful and efficient. Singer Karen Burlingame worked beyond the limits of my expectations while she was on Hilton Head Island, playing the lead in *The Sound of Music*. Brigit McQuay, Carmen Hawkins and Lori Soergel kept my world spinning while I attempted to keep all my balls in the air. Miles McSweeney; Lynn Felder; Jolyn Bowler; and Mickey, Zoe and Loet Vos each tolerated hearing of my progress throughout the project. Frank Malloy of Charleston was responsible for finding the *andrinka* design on the cover. Lewis Hammet was of immeasurable assistance coming in at the eleventh hour to pull everything together.

Finally, for her support and assistance in the face of all enemies—foreign, domestic and internal—my most heartfelt thanks goes out to a gracious critic and unrelenting editor, Ruth Gaul Killhour, my dear old friend.

INTRODUCTION

The first Africans to settle in South Carolina arrived with five hundred Spanish settlers from Santo Domingo in 1526. Within six months, the Lowcountry environment saw the well-ordered hierarchy of the strutting Spaniards turned into a tempestuous caldron of secession and rebellion. The Roman Catholic tendency to justify whatever means were necessary to propagate the Faith failed to win for them the hearts and minds of the local natives or the Africans. Not surprisingly, the Africans became fast friends with their brothers yoked by common oppression. When Indian attacks finally drove out the one hundred and fifty Spanish survivors, the Africans decided to remain in the Lowcountry with their native allies.

Little is known of the first settlers in what would soon be South Carolina. The trail is cold. Academicians can't even agree on the location of the settlement. But I enjoy imagining that it was the Africans' adaptability, combined with a friendly environment and friendly indigenous people, which enabled them to thrive and prosper. I also can't resist being amused by the fact that African-Americans, these self-emancipated men and women and descendants of color, had been living in the South for four generations when the Europeans finally gained a foot-hold at Jamestown.

The flip side of this story is less amusing. "Historians" (those not raised in South Carolina) have all but ignored this profound event and the African-American culture that it initiated. The boundary crossed by the Native Americans and the Africans during the Chicora incident was the spiritual foundation of this nation's African-American tradition. It is ethnically hybrid, daring, racially cooperative, revolutionary and flexible to the natural environment. I can think of few traditions more worthy of the full embrace of my pride. Gullah culture—or the remnants of it that we are fortunate to record—is still the oldest known African-American culture that survives in this country. For hundreds of years it was nearly ignored into extinction. Now, ironically, public interest and enthusiasm in this society's proud "Africa-ness" is swiftly pushing the language into oblivion.

But it is the nature of language to be fluid. And while Gullah's popularity may be reshaping the language, it's only natural that cultures adapt to other cultures with which they share the same environment. This same mutability, however, only underscores the need for preserving any material passed down from their elder speakers.

Though my editor blames the popularity of Pat Conroy's books for bringing Daufuskie Island and its Gullah culture into the 20th century, to my jaded middle-aged mind, it seemed as inevitable as the tides. When Albert H. Stoddard recorded the stories he learned as child a few years before his death, he reported that the intrusions that had entered Gullah since his youth had rendered the language almost incomprehensible to his ancient ear.

Albert H. Stoddard (1872-1954) grew up on Daufuskie Island, South Carolina, the remote Sea Island that was subjected to the public eye after Pat Conroy's 1972 novel *The Water Is Wide* and the subsequent movie *Conrak*. Mr. Stoddard planted sea-island cotton on Melrose, his family homestead, as generations before him had done. Today, Melrose is an elegant seaside retreat for members and guests with soft hands and deep pockets.

Mr. Stoddard was not a stereotypical Southern Gentleman after the War Between the States. He was a man for whom borders were not obstacles. He had relatives and business interests in both the North and the South; his native Sea Island bordered the sea and the land; and all across his country's southern half, the border between Africa and Europe twisted and coiled like a trapped black snake.

Albert H. Stoddard was a direct descendent of David Mongin, who was granted the island in 1740 by George II for subduing pirates. When John Stoddard married the orphaned Mary Mongin, the grandiose ceremony took place in the American Embassy in Paris. The family fortune prospered by the sea-island cotton. But Albert recognized another form of island wealth as well. In their manners and speech, the people of Daufuskie shared a treasured part of their essential "Africa-ness"—their Afrique—with a young boy who would grow to make a cherished contribution to their folklore.

From infancy, Mr. Stoddard's inquiring mind absorbed the scents and sounds, the rich color and ancient character of the island and its black residents. He was likely cared for by an older Gullah woman and thereby received African-American values first hand. The early caretakers of a majority of upper-middle-class youngsters were experienced African-American women. Until the recent generations, most "well bred" white Southerners were initially influenced by African-American ideals of behavior, propriety and language.

For many years, the South has enjoyed a reputation of politeness and hospitality. As a child, I was told that this advantage was due to the South's close economic ties with Great Britain. This myth was also used to explain the origin of both the dialect of white Southerners and the language of the Gullahs. I had accepted this as fact. But working on this project has led me to speculate that perhaps there was less influence from England than there was from Africa.

Hospitality, for example, does not strike me as a British personality trait that would have been apparent—much less admired enough to emulate—in a British colony three hundred years ago. Yet, in these tales, I notice standards of behavior exhibiting uncommon civility. Even if one character is about to eat his neighbor, he feels compelled to "mek e mannus"—address with appropriate politeness—his upcoming meal. I suspect that this kind behavior would be welcome in places other than the Sea Islands. I cannot prove that Southern morals and manners are of African origin. I can only direct your attention to the phenomena that suggests such a conclusion. It's the polite thing to do.

The Sea Islands fulfill so many mythic needs for modern culture— green vegetation, warm winters, ocean beaches, relative isolation and a healthy supply of potentially deadly and tasty creatures. These are also some of the environmental elements that allowed Gullah culture to develop. The stories in this volume illustrate the symbiotic relationship of a unique people to an environment that nurtures both mystery and abundance.

But the prime mover of culture is language. It gives shape to unique ideas and visa versa. This book and tape are a brave attempt to entertain more Americans while exposing them to a very ancient wisdom. Culturally speaking, we are all African-Americans. Africanism, in fact, could possibly be the very heart of American culture. The West African tradition of having a tribal griot, singer of the tribe's history, became the itinerant bluesman who was the catalyst in the development of American popular culture. The Black Church, anxious for legitimacy by European standards, suppressed his ritual significance and, ironically, empowered it. This tradition is so strong and resonant that it gave rise to a cultural revolution that is still changing the world today. I would be surprised if Rock ever died.

Folks like Joel Chandler Harris, Du Bose Heyward, Lydia Parrish, Lucy Garrison, Ambrose Gonzales and Albert H. Stoddard were aware of the value of our African traditions as they were cradled in the Gullah language, literature and music. Perhaps they knew something others did not; when an ethnic language (even a hybrid one) begins to fade, other cultural elements often follow. Such is the nature of things.

My primary motive in translating and presenting these stories in this manner is to make them as accessible as possible to as many people as possible. Most previous books concerning Gullah language and culture were either in difficult-to-read transliterations of the oral forms or in scholarly studies. Both forms tend to limit the accessibility of the folklore.

Because of my conviction, folklore is for the "folks," and is, therefore, past popular culture; it occurred to me that I should do what I could to bring the "folks" into contact with this very special body of literature.

The rich material that is represented by the following selection was chosen because it was the most comprehensible out of the corpus that Mr. Stoddard left behind. Most of these folktales, or myths, are known in the brain trade as "etiological." "Etiological" is the silliest sounding word that mythologists could come up with to label stories that explain the causes, or origins, of phenomena. A prime example of an etiological myth is the first story in this collection, "Man Get E Adam Apple" ("Man Gets His Adams Apple"). It's the story of the origin of the Adams apple, the lump in a man's throat.

An interesting characteristic of the language is it's use of gender-inclusive pronouns. Linguists and philologists have so far been unable to come up with a set of pronouns for American English that is not sexually exclusive. "He/she" and "him/her" are unwieldy to even the most maniacal of the politically correct. In Gullah, however, "he," "she" and "it" are all expressed by the free morpheme "e." The objective pronouns "him," "her" and "it" are all expressed by the free morpheme "um." Watch out OED! What a beautifully simple concept: Make words shorter to enhance their meaning. It's almost . . . American.

I had doubted the current theory that Gullah is a language (as opposed to a dialect) until I began working on this project. I now fully support that concept. It's uniqueness is evident in its syntax, inflection and prosodic signals. I also suspect that the classic myth that Gullah borrowed heavily from earlier forms of English is spurious and probably racist. The process, I contend, was reversed. It is unlikely that early Gullahs were exposed to enough complex and archaic English words for them to naturally absorb them into their everyday communication. It is more likely that when English speakers heard Africans use a word like "tippity" to mean "dislike," they reasoned that the Africans meant to say "antipathy." English people merely assumed the slaves were trying to do the only reasonable thing, speaking English, they simply weren't very good at. A phenomenal conceit, to be sure, but one that was all too common in the souls of empire-builders.

I am grateful to the Gullah language for teaching me that Europeans didn't civilize a formless population of savages. They only enslaved a variety of cultures. Perhaps the most ironic indemnification of that forced migration was that the savages whom the Europeans enslaved ended up civilizing the Europeans. We don't owe a debt to our

African-American heritage for having imposed the horrendous institution of slavery on some people in the past; we owe our African-American heritage a debt of gratitude for it's valuable gifts to our cultural character today, not the least of which is the very soul of our nation.

As our standards of conduct and value systems erode, perhaps we need to hang on tighter to the roots of our common culture rather than attempt to legislate mythologies based on flawed precidents (such as "the good old days"). I suggest that it is not a coincidence that, while we are fast losing touch with the evidence of our common African-American heritage, we are noticing a proportional loss of what some have termed "American Family Values."

Will Killhour
April 15, 1995
Hilton Head Island

PREFACE

Clever Eshu

Once all the orisha, neglected by men on earth, went hungry. Obaluaiye attempted to terrify men into sacrificing, but they became too depressed in their sickness to care what happened to them. Shango's wrathful thunderbolts only made men deceive themselves into thinking other responsible for their misfortunes. Ogun tried his skill in hunting, but he couldn't kill enough to feed everyone; and the fish provided by Shango's wives were scarcely sufficient for their own children.

Eshu, youngest and cleverest of the orisha, went to visit ancient Yemonja, the profoundest of them all. The mother of the waters said, "Men no longer fear death. Give them something to yearn for, then, out of gratitude, they will gladly sacrifice in order to go on living."

"I can conceive of only one possible source of such hope," Eshu said, thanking her for her counsel.

Eshu then went to call on his very special friend Orunmila. "What you suggest makes good sense," said Orunmila, "I'm amazed that you thought of it. Certain monkeys have told me of such a hope, a secret lodged in the four corners of the universe. But although I sense new sap rising in me,

I'm much too tired to move about just now. I'll have to send you off to do that errand for me. Go east, west, north and south. From each direction take four parts of this secret. I'll put them together here, and we shall see what we shall see."

"Promise to feed me first whenever you sit down to eat," said the wily Eshu, "and I'll be your messenger."

"Of course," said Orunmila, "don't accuse me of bad manners."

When Eshu returned, Orunmila looked at what he had brought and said, "Palm fronds shall be the thatch to repair the breach through which disaster leaks into the king's house as into the meanest hovel. Palm nuts shall feed the orisha. Palm kernels shall be the words from which shall sprout a forest of meanings." So saying, he planted the sixteen parts of the secret in his head, and they burgeoned forth as Ifa, the force of divination.

"Now go down to earth and find me interpreters," said Orunmila, "priests who can open my sixteen windows to let men take a peek at smooth running destiny. And when they see all the lesser evils that can be avoided, the obstructions that can be cleared from their paths, they will be eager to make sacrifices to all of us. Between earth and sky shall flow sweet words then, fresh blood and renewed strength to overcome adversity."

"Don't forget my dash - my tip," said Eshu.

"O no, my friend, you shall be entitled to the first portion of every meal. Men shall not fail to give you one for the road."

"In that case," said Eshu enigmatically, "I'll always be traveling. Good-bye. I'm on my way like the starving man who slings the sack of necessity over his shoulder and bolts for freedom. I know my fate without reading it - always on the move, that's me. But know this, my very special friend, I love discord, disobedience and change better than I love palm nuts. So I shall take every occasion to make the world dance to my music, and be fed double for my pains. Twice to get out of trouble and once to get in, that's *my* secret."

Orisha: The Gods of Yorubaland
Judith Illsley Gleason

xvii

CONTENTS

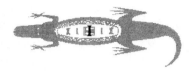

45-A1

MAN GETS HIS ADAMS APPLE

1   When Father first made the world, it was all covered with water, and it was not a fitting place for either man or creature to live.

Father saw it wasn't a fitting place so he made a canal, a ditch, and a drain to drain off the water. And when the earth was dry, he planted grass and all kinds of herbs and things to be food for man and beast.

Father saw that there was not yet light upon the earth for things to see to get about. So he made the sun for the day, and the moonshine and the stars to be light in the night.

Father made one good garden and he put all kinds of things in there. Then he found out he had so much business that he didn't have time to care for the

45-A1

MAN GIT E ADAM APPLE

1   When Farrer fus mek de wul, e bin all kibber ober wid watuh, en e ain bin no fitten place fuh eeder man uh eeder creetur fuh lib.

Farrer see e ain bin no fitten place en e mek canal en ditch en quatuh dreen fuh dreen de watuh off, en when de yut done dry e tek en plant grass en all kine uh beyobs en ting fuh be bittle fuh man en beas.

Farrer yet see dey ain no light puntop de yut fuh ting fuh see fuh get bout, so e mek de sun fuh de day, en de moonshine en de sta fuh be light een de night.

Farrer mek one good ga-a-den en e put all kine ub uh ting een dey. Den e come fuh fine out e had summuch uh binnis tell e ain ha time fuh mine de ga-a-den, en e does wa' one hans fuh ten de ga-a-garden, and he wanted a helper to tend the garden for him.

5   Father took some of the dirt in the garden and he made it into the shape of the man. Then he breathed his breath into a nostril, and he made him come alive.

When the man came alive, Father told him his name was Adam and his job was to tend the garden for Father.

Adam tended the garden and tried to do his work faithfully, but Adam spent so much time working around the house and cooking his food that, when the June rains came, he wasn't able to keep up with his work.

Also, his pure loneliness got him down. He had no one to talk with and keep him company.

Adam went to Father and displayed the proper manners. Afterwards, Father asked what he wanted.

10   Adam said to Father, "Please, sir, Father, I try to do my work faithfully, but it takes me so much time to sweep, work around the house, and cook my food that I have not been able to be in the field enough. And the June grass is

den fuh um.

5   Farrer tek some de dut een de ga-a-den en e mek um een de shape ub uh man, en e breeze e bret een e noshril en e mek um come libe.

When e come libe Farrer tell um say e name duh Adam en e fuh ten de ga-a-den fuh um.

Adam ten de ga-a-den en try fuh do e wuk faitful, but Adam hads summuch uh time fuh min' roun e house en cook e bittle tell, when dem June rain come Adam ain bin able fuh keep up wid e wuk.

Den gen de p'yo lonedly git um down. E ain hads no one fuh talk tuh en fuh be comp'ny fuh um.

Adam gone tuh Farrer en at e done mek e mannus, Farrer ax um wuh e does wa'.

10   Adam tell Farrer say, "Please, suh Farrer, uh does try fuh do muh wuk faitful, but it tek me summuch uh time fuh sweep en ten roun de house en fuh cook muh bittle tell uh ain able fuh be een de fiel nuf en dem June grass duh gwine git head uh me. Den, suh Farrer, de p'yo lonedly done git me down. Please, suh Farrer, see ef yo

2

going to get ahead of me. Then, sir, Father, pure loneliness has me feeling depressed. Please, sir, Father, see if you could get another worker to help me."

Father told Adam he would see what he could do for him, and Adam turned and started to go back to work.

Father called out to him, "Adam!"

Adam turned and went back to Father. And Father made him fall asleep. When he was asleep, Father took one of his smallest ribs and made a woman. When Adam woke up, the woman was there beside him.

Father said to Adam, "Adam, this is your Eve. I made her to be company for you, to take care of the house, to cook your food, and to help you in the field when she has time.

15   Adam took Eve home with him. The woman was help enough to Adam and was good company for him, but she loved to talk a lot.

She didn't care who she talked to as long he'd listen to her. She talked so much that Adam had

couldn' gie me nedder hans fuh help me."

Farrer tell Adam say e would uh see wuh e could uh do bout um, en Adam tun en sta-a-t fuh go back tuh e wuk.

Farrer call um, "Adam!"

Adam tun en e gone back tuh Farrer, en Farrer tek um en mek um fuh drop sleep, en when e duh sleep Farrer tek out one e leases rib en mek ooman, en when Adam wake up de ooman dey dey side um.

Farrer tell Adam say, "Adam, dis yuh duh Ebe. Uh mek um fuh be comp'ny fuh yo en fuh mine de house en fuh cook yo bittle en fuh help yo een de fiel when e does ha time."

15   Adam tek Ebe home wid um en de ooman is bin nuf uh help tuh Adam en e bin good comp'ny fuh um, but e berry lub compersation.

E dunk'yer who e duh talk tuh dis so e'd yeddy tur um. E talk summuch tell Adam hads fuh lef de house dis fuh res' e yays, en e tell de gal say, "Summuch uh compersation duh gwine git yuh een trouble one uh dese days."

to leave the house to rest his ears. He said to the girl, "Too much conversation is going to get you into trouble one of these days."

One time Father had to go into town on business. He came into the garden and called on Adam. He said to him, "Adam, I have to go into town on business and I will be gone two or three days. You and Eve take charge of the garden and tend it well while I'm away. Anything that is here in the garden is yours to use, except one thing. You are not to touch the young apple tree that is bearing. If you touch that tree, you will surely die."

Adam said to Father, "Yes sir, Father." And he turned and went back to work.

The serpent was in the grass and he heard everything Father told Adam and, when Adam had gone back to the field, he went to Eve. He sweet talked her by saying, "Good morning." She said, "Good morning, sir."

20   The serpent told Eve that they had an especially pretty garden and that Father must think well of them because of all their hard work.

One time Farrer hads fuh go town on binnis en e come een de ga-a-den en call Adam en tell um say, "Adam, uh gots fuh go town on binnis en uh gwine be gone two tree day. You en Ebe fuh tek chage de ga-a-den en mine um good while uh dey-dey, en ennyting wuh dey een de ga-a-den duh younna fuh nuse, scusin tuh one ting. Da nyung apple tree wuh dis duh beer younna ain fuh tetch dat. Sho es yo tetch dat, yo duh gwine dead."

Adam tell Farrer say, "Yes, suh, Farrer." En e tun en gone back tuh e wuk.

De sarpint bin eed de grass en e yeddy wud Farrer tell Adam, en when Adam done gone een de fiel e gone tuh Ebe. E put on e sweet mout en e tell um say, "Good mawnin." Suh Ebe tell um say, "Good mawnin, suh."

20   De sarpint tell Ebe say dey hads one pooty ga-a-den, en Farrer mus be tink well uh dem fuh do all uh da ha-a-d wuk.

Ebe say, "E is tink well uh we. E duh gwine town en e tun de whole ga-a-den ober tuh we fuh we fuh we fuh tek ennyting wuh diddy scusin tuh one lone ting. De

Eve said, "He does think well of us. He has gone to town and turned the whole garden over to us. We can take anything that is here except one thing." The serpent asked her, "What is that?" Eve told him that it was the young apple which was the first to bear fruit. "If we touch that we are going to die."

The serpent laughed, "S-s-s-s. Father told you that because he knows that it is the sweetest thing in the garden and he wants it for himself. Take one and taste it. He isn't going to kill you. Father isn't going to miss one tiny little old apple."

Eve told him, no sir, she wasn't going to take an apple; she doesn't want to die.

The serpent sweet-talked her and sweet-talked her until Eve took one of the apples and tasted it. The bite sweetened her mouth very much.

25   As soon as she chewed the first mouthful, Adam came out of the field and Eve put the apple behind her back.

Adam said, "Girl, what is that you are hiding behind your

sarpint ax um, "Wuh dat?" en Ebe tell um duh da nyung apple wuh dis duh beer fuh de fus. "Ef we tetch dat we duh gwine dead."

De sarpint laugh, "S-s-s-s. Farrer tell yo dat case e know duh de sweetes ting een de ga-a-den en e want um fuh e self. Tek one en tase um. E ain duh gwine dead yo. Farrer ain duh gwine miss one leetle ole apple."

Ebe tell um, no suh, him ain duh gwine tek no apple; him ain wa' dead.

De sarpint sweet mout um en sweet-mout um tell Ebe tek one de apple en ta'se um. En de ting sweeten e mout tummuch.

25   Dis e bin uh nyam de fus moutfull, Adam come out de fiel en Ebe chook de apple behime e back.

Adam say, "Gal, wuh da yo duh hide behime your back?" Ebe say, "E ain duh nuttin, suh." Adam say, "E is duh suppin. Show me wuh yo got."

Ebe pull out de apple, en when Adam shum e holler, "Gal, trow dat ting way fo yo dead. Fuh whuf fuh yo gone done de ting Farrer tell yo yo en fuh de?"

back?" Eve said, "I'm not doing anything, sir."

Adam said, "You are doing something. Show me what you have."

Eve pulled out the apple, and when Adam saw it he shouted. "Girl, throw the thing away before you die. Why have you done the very thing that Father told you not to do?"

Eve said it wasn't her that took the apple. It was the serpent that made her take the apple.

Again Adam told her to throw the thing away, but Eve sweet-talked Adam into taking a bite of the apple.

30   Father didn't leave for town as soon as he thought. He was waiting for the tide to turn so his oarsmen wouldn't have such a hard pull against the tide, and he took a walk in the garden.

Just as Adam took his first big bite of the apple, Father called him, "Adam!"

Adam didn't have time to chew the apple and tried to swallow it. The bit went down in his throat

Ebe tell um say ain duh him tek de apple, duh de sarpint mek um tek de apple.

Adam gen tell um fuh trow de ting way, but Ebe tun en sweet-mout um tell Adam tek one bite de apple.

30   Farrer ain bin gone town soon es e tought. E bin uh wait fuh de tide fuh tun so e oasmen wouldn' uh had summuch uh ha-a-d pullin fuh go gen tide, en e tek uh walk en gone een de ga-a-den.

Dis Adam tek e fus big bite de apple, Farrer call um, "Adam!"

Adam ain bin ha time fuh n'yam de apple en e try fuh swaller um. De ting gone down een e trote en come up, gone down een e trote en come up. En ebber sence dat, man bin ha Adam apple.

Farrer git bex fuh dem do wuh e tell dem dey ain fuh do, tell e run all two uh dem out de ga-a-den, en Adam hads fuh tek up new groun en wuhk so hahd fuh mek out, en Farrer bin dat bex tell fuh punish dem e mek out fuh git een dem hay en skeeter en san' nat en all kine ub uh ting fuh bodderation man en beas.

and came up, went down in his
throat and came up. And ever since
that day, men has had an Adams
apple.

Father got angry because
they didn't do what he told them to
do, so he ran the two of them out of
the garden. Adam had to settle on
less fertile ground that required
more labor to make it produce. But
Father was so furious he sent mos-
quitoes and gnats to get in their
hair and all kinds of things to
annoy man and beast.

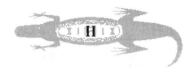

45-A2

45-A2

BROTHER PARTRIDGE OUTHIDES BROTHER RABBIT

BUH PARTRIDGE OUTHIDES BUH RABBIT

1   One time Brother Rabbit was walking about just for the pleasure of it and he met up with Brother Partridge who was taking his pleasure too.

They started talking and sat upon a log. Soon, the talk turned to hiding. Brother Rabbit told Brother Partridge that he could outhide Brother Partridge. Brother Partridge said, "he couldn't." Brother Rabbit said, "he could." Brother Partridge said, "he couldn't." Brother Rabbit said, "he could."

Brother Partridge said, "Brother Rabbit, there is no need for us to settle this dispute this way. The way to do it is for you to hide yourself and when you are well hidden, you whoop. When I hear you whoop, I'll go hunt for you.

1   One time Buh Rabbit bin uh walk bout bin uh pledger e self en e meet up wid Buh Pa'tridge bin uh pledger e self.

Dem sta-a-t fuh talk, en dem set down puntop one log. Turrecly de talk gone tun puntop hide. Buh Rabbit tell Buh Pa'tridge e kin out hide Buh Pa'tridge. Buh Pa'tridge tell um say, "e yent." Buh Rabbit say, "e is." Buh Pa'tridge tell um, "e yent." Buh Rabbit say, "e is."

Buh Pa'tridge say, "Buh Rabbit, dey ain no cayjon fuh we fuh set yuh duh sputefy. De way fuh yo do, yo go go hide yo self en when yo done hide good, yo whoop, en when uh yeddy yo whoop uh'l go hunt yo. Den duh my time fo hide."

Then it will be my turn to hide."

Brother Rabbit went down and hid himself well underneath a bush where nobody could see him. And when he was well hidden, he whooped. When Brother Partridge heard him whoop, he went to hunt for him.

5   Brother Partridge was the kind of man who could hide himself so nobody could see him. But Brother Rabbit was so scared that somebody might come upon him without him seeing him coming that he kept his eye open to look all about from the bush and see if anybody was coming.

When Brother Partridge heard Brother Rabbit whoop, he went to hunt for him. The first thing that Brother Partridge saw was Brother Rabbit's big eye shining out of the bush.

He said, "Go along, Brother Rabbit, anybody could see you. Your big eye shines a mile."

Then it was Brother Partridge's turn to hide himself.

Brother Partridge told Brother Rabbit the exact spot where he was going to hide himself. He

Buh Rabbit gone down en hide e self good on'neet one bush whey no body couldn' ur shum, en when e done hide good, e whoop. When Buh Pa'tridge yeddy um whoop e gone fuh hunt um.

5   Buh Pa'tridge duh one man lukka dis yer—e could uh hide e self en no body couldn' ur shum. But Buh Rabbit so skayed say somebody might uh come puntop um en ketch um en him no does shum shum when dem does comin, tell e duh keep duh run e yie out de bush duh look all erbout fuh see ef anybody duh comin.

When Buh Pa'tridge yeddy Buh Rabbit whoop, e gone fuh hunt um. Fus ting Buh Pa'tridge see duh Buh Rabbit big yie duh shine out de bush.

E say, "Gullong, Buh Rabbit, anybody could uh see yo big yie duh shine uh mile."

Now duh Buh Pa'tridge time fuh hide e self.

Buh Pa'tridge tell Buh Rabbit de berry dizac spot e duh gwine hide e self. E gone down dat dizac spot en hide e self, en when e done hide e self, e whoop.

11

went down to that exact spot and he hid himself. When he had hidden himself, he whooped.

10   And when Brother Rabbit heard him whoop, he went hunting for him.

He went down to that exact spot; he didn't see Brother Partridge. He looked all about; he didn't see Brother Partridge . He got on his hands and knees and turned all the leaves and things searching all about, all about for a long time, yet he didn't see Brother Partridge.

By and by, he got tired and stood up on his feet and said, "Brother Partridge, I give up."

Brother Partridge said, "Brother Rabbit if you give up, move from on top of me so I can get up."

10   En when Buh Rabbit yeddy um whoop, e gone fuh hunt um.

E gone down dat dizac spot; e ain see Buh Pa'tridge. E look all erbout; e ain see Buh Pa'tridge. E git on e han en knee, en e tun all de leaf en ting en e sarch all erbout, all erbout, long time, e yet ain see Buh Pa'tridge.

Bum by, e git tire, e stan up on e foots en say, "Buh Pa'tridge, uh gibs up."

Buh Pa'tridge say. "Do, Buh Rabbit, ef yo gibs up, moob fuhm puntop me so uh kin git up."

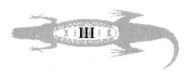

44-A1

HOW BROTHER HOUND GOT HIS LONG SNOUT

1   When Father first made Brother Hound, his mouth didn't look like it looks now. It was round like his eye, only bigger.

Brother Rabbit was in his rice field harvesting his rice and the sun got very hot. Brother Rabbit left his field and went up on the flood bank where there were some bushes. He sat down underneath a bush in the shade and began to whistle.

In those days Brother Rabbit and Brother Hound were good friends. Brother Hound came along and heard Brother Rabbit whistle. He said to Brother Rabbit, "I wish I could whistle like you."

Brother Rabbit told him his mouth didn't look like it could whistle. "A round mouth isn't for

44-A1

HOW BUH HOUN GIT E LONG MOUT

1   When Farrer fus bin mek Buh Houn, e mout ain stan sukka yo shum stan now. E bin roun sukka e yie, ondly e bin mo bigger.

Buh Rabbit bin een e rice fiel duh habes e rice en de sun git berry hot en Buh Rabbit lef e fiel en gone up on de flood bank whey some bush dey, en e set down onneet one bush een de shade en biggin fuh whistle.

Dem days Buh Rabbit en Buh Houn bin good frens. Buh Houn come long en yeddy Buh Rabbit duh whistle. E say, "Buh Rabbit, uh wish uh could uh whistle lukka younna."

Buh Rabbit tell um say e mout ain stan fuh whiste. "Roun mout ain fuh whistle. Ef yo had long mout lukka mine yo could uh whistling. If you had a long mouth like mine you could whistle."

5   Brother Hound told Brother Rabbit that he wished he had a long mouth so he could whistle.

Brother Rabbit told Brother Hound that he could if he gave him a long mouth.

Brother Hound asked Brother Rabbit, if he gives him a long mouth, is it going to hurt him?

Brother Rabbit told him that it wouldn't hurt him when he got his long mouth.

Brother Hound said, "Brother Rabbit, give me a long mouth and teach me how to whistle."

10   Brother Rabbit had a reap hook with him that they had been cutting rice with. He told Brother Hound to hold his head as high as he could, to shut his eyes tight, and to draw a long breath.

Brother Hound held his head as high as he could, shut his eyes, and drew a long breath. Brother Rabbit took the reap hook in both hands, brought it down on top of Brother Hound's mouth, and

whistle."

5   Buh Houn tell Buh Rabbit say e wish e ha uh long mout en e could uh whistle.

Buh Rabbit tell Buh Houn say e could uh gie um long mout.

Buh Houn ax Buh Rabbit say ef e does gie um long mout es e gwine hut um.

Buh Rabbit tell um say e ain hut um none tall when e git e long mout.

Buh Houn say, "Do, Buh Rabbit, gie me long mout en teach me fuh whistle."

10   Buh Rabbit had e reap hook wid um whey e bin uh cut rice with. E tell Buh Houn fuh hole e head high es e kin is, en e fuh shet e yie tight, en e fuh draw long bret.

Buh Houn hole e head high es e kin is, en e shet e yie, en e draw uh long bret. Buh Rabbit tek de reap hook een all two e hans en come down puntop Buh Houn mout en cut um mos' back tuh e yays.

When Buh Houn feel Buh Rabbit reap hook duh cut um, e

cut it almost back to his ears.

When Brother Hound felt Brother Rabbit's reap hook cut him, he yelped, "Wow!"

He opened his eyes to see what Brother Rabbit was doing. He saw Brother Rabbit looking at him and laughing. He tried to talk to Brother Rabbit but his mouth hurt so much that all he could say was, "Wow, Wow." He started to approach Brother Rabbit but Brother Rabbit thought he was coming to hurt him so he ran away.

Brother Hound ran after Brother Rabbit to try to talk to him but all he could say was, "Wow, Wow." Ever since that day, when Brother Hound sees Brother Rabbit, he runs after him and yelps, "Wow, Wow, Wow, Wow, Wow." And every time Brother Hound holds his head high, like when he look at the moon, he remembers how Brother Rabbit's reap hook hurt him, so he yelps, "Wow-wow-wow-wow-ough-ough-o-o-o."

holler, "Wow!"

E open e yie fuh see wuh Buh Rabbit duh do. E see Buh Rabbit duh stan dey duh laugh puntop um. E try fuh talk tuh Buh Rabbit but e mout hut um summuch tell all e could uh say duh, "Wow, Wow." E sta-a-t fuh go tuh Buh Rabbit en Buh Rabbit tink say e duh comin fuh hut um en e run off.

Buh Houn run at Buh Rabbit en does try fuh talk tur um but all e could uh say duh, "Wow, Wow." Ebber sence dat when Buh Houn see Buh Rabbit, e does run um en e holler, "Wow, Wow, Wow, Wow." En ebby time Buh Houn does hole e head high, lukka when e does look puntop de moon, e mek um membunce uh how Buh Rabbit reap hook hut um, en e holler, "Wow-wow-wow-wow-ough-ough-o-o-o."

44-A2

HOW BROTHER HOUND GOT HIS LONG TONGUE

1   When Brother Hound was first made with his little mouth that was round like his eye, he had no use for a long tongue. But after Brother Rabbit made him have a long mouth, he wanted a long tongue that could hang out of his mouth to catch air and cool him when he was hot.

He saw Brother Fox and Brother Coon and plenty of other creatures who could hang their tongues out of their mouths, and every time he saw them it made him want a long tongue more and more.

Brother Alligator lived in the water and didn't have a need to hang his tongue out to cool itself, yet Brother Alligator had a long tongue that could come way out of his mouth.

44-A2

HOW BUH HOUN GIT E LONG TONGUE

1   When Buh Houn bin fus mek wid e leetle mout roun sukka e yie e ain hads no nuse fuh no long tongue, but at Buh Rabbit mek um fuh ha long mout e does wa' long tongue wuh kin hang out e mout fuh ketch de ear fuh cool um when e does hot.

E see Buh Fox en Buh Coon en nuf uh dem tarrer creeter wuh kin hang dem tongue out dem mout, en ebby time e does shum e mek um mo en mo wa' long tongue.

B'Allegetter lib een de watuh en e don' hads no need fuh hang e tongue out fuh cool e self, en B'Allegetter ha long tongue whey kin come way out e mut.

One big dry drought come puntop de lan en all de watuh hole en ting dry up, en de hole befo

A big dry drought came upon the land and all the water holes and things had dried up, and the hole in front of Brother Alligator dried up and left no water for him to go in.

5 Brother Alligator started to go to a creek a distance from his house where there was always water. He had gone halfway across a big field under a very hot sun when Brother Alligator came to a bush and went underneath it in the shade to rest, and fell asleep.

Brother Hound came along and saw Brother Alligator there asleep with his tongue hanging way out of his mouth, and he was panting his breath.

Brother Hound crept up on Brother Alligator, and he caught Brother Alligator's tongue in his mouth and he bit it off close to Brother Alligator's teeth before he woke up.

Brother Hound ran off with Brother Alligator's tongue until he got off a safe distant. Then he held Brother Alligator's tongue to his own tongue until they grew together. Ever since that day, Brother Hound has had a long tongue that

B'Allegetter house dry up en ain lef no watuh fuh e go een.

5 B'Allegetter sta-a-t fuh go tuh one crick a distant fuhm e house whey watuh always does dey. When e does gwine e haffuh cross on big fiel en de sun dey berry hot, en when B'Allegetter come tuh one bushish e gone on'neet um een de shade fuh res e self, en e drop sleep.

Buh Houn come long en e see B'Allegetter dey-dey duh sleep wid e tongue duh hang way out e mout, en e duh panch e bret.

Buh Houn creep up puntop B'Allegetter en ketch B'Allegetter tongue een e mout en bite um off close tuh B'Allegetter teet fo e wak up.

Buh Houn run off wid B'Allegetter tongue tell e git off uh safe distant, den e hole B'Allegetter tongue tuh him tongue tell dem done grow tugedder. Ebber sence dat, Buh Houn ha long tongue wuh kin hang way out e mout fuh ketch de ear, en B'Allegetter ha leetle shawt no-count tongue wuh ca' come out e mout.

B'Allegetter always does wa' to git e tongue back en a leabe any could hang way out his mouth to catch the air, and Brother Alligator has had a little short, good-for-nothing tongue that can't come out of his mouth.

Brother Alligator has always wanted to get his tongue back. He will leave anything else to go after Brother Hound in hopes of getting his tongue back.

ting else fuh go at Buh Houn een de hopes uh gitten e tongue back.

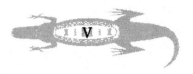

44-A3

HOW BROTHER WASP GOT HIS SMALL WAIST

1   In the beginning, Brother Wasp's waist wasn't little the way you see it now. It was as big as anybody's waist. The way Brother Wasp came to get his little waist, he was walking along the road and he saw Brother Skeeter hoeing potatoes in his field.

He said to him, "Good morning, Brother Skeeter, how are all of yours?" Brother Skeeter answered him saying, "We are all making out very well, thank God. How are all of yours?"

Brother Wasp told him that all of them were there, thank God.

Brother Wasp leaned himself against the fence and they began to talk. Brother Wasp said, "Brother Skeeter, it looks like you've got as very fine crop of potatoes in your

44-A3

HOW BUH WAS' GET E SMALL WAIST

1   Een de fus off sta-a-tin Buh Was' wais ain bin leetle lukka how yo shum stan now. E bin big ez anybody wais. En de way Buh Was' come fuh git e leetle wais e bin uh walk long de road en e see Buh Skeeter duh hoe tutter een e fiel.

E tell um say, "Good mawnin, Buh Skeeter, how all uh younna?" Buh Skeeter gie um answer say, "We all duh mekkin out berry well, tank Gawd. How all uh younna?"

Buh Was' tell um say all uh dem dey-dey tank Gawd.

Buh Was' lean e self on de fench en dem biggin talk. Buh Was' say, "Buh Skeeter, e look luk yo got uh berry fine crop uh tutter een yo fiel dis ear."

5   Buh Skeeter tell um say,

field this year.

5 Brother Skeeter said, "Yes, this is the best crop of potatoes I ever raised in my life. They are all fine potatoes."

Brother Wasp told him that it was fine for him to have such good potatoes.

Brother Skeeter told him that he did have good potatoes, but if he wanted to see truly big potatoes, he should go and see his Pa's field. Everyone of them was a big, fine potato. There wasn't a little potato in his Pa's whole field.

Brother Wasp asked Brother Skeeter how big the potatoes were in his Pa's field.

Brother Skeeter was barefoot. He put his foot on top of the potato hill and pulled up his pantaloon leg. Then he said to Brother Wasp, "Brother Wasp, do you see my leg here?"

10 Brother Wasp told him, yes, he saw it.

Brother Skeeter said, "Brother Wasp, every one of the potatoes in my Pa's field is just as big as my leg is here. There isn't a

"Yeh, dis de bes crop uh tutter uh ebber raise een muh life. All duh good fine tutter."

Buh Was' tell um say da's fine fuh e ha sischa good tutter.

Buh Skeeter tell um say e ha good tutter fuh true, but ef e wa' see big tutter fuh true, e fuh go een e Pa fiel. Ebby one dem duh big, fine tutter, ent uh leetle tutter dey een e whole Pa fiel.

Buh Was' ax Buh Skeeter how big de tutter dey een e Pa fiel.

Buh Skeeter bin bayfoot en e put e foot puntop de tutter hill en pull up e pantloon laig, en e tell Buh Was' say, "Buh Was', yo see muh laig yuh so?"

10 Buh Was' tell um say, yeh, e shum.

Buh Skeeter tell um say, "Buh Was', ebby one de tutter een muh Pa fiel dis big ez muh laig yuh so. Ent uh leetle tutter dey een e Pa whole fiel."

Buh Was' look puntop Buh Skeeter duh stan up dey so biggety duh show e leetle dry bone shank fuh show how big de tutter een e Pa fiel dey, en e tink say ef de tutter

little potato there in my Pa's whole field."

Brother Wasp looked upon Brother Skeeter standing up there so proud of himself showing his little dry bone shank to show how big the potatoes were in his Pa's field, and he thought that if the potatoes weren't any bigger than that, then there was a powerfully poor chance of doing any eating, and he burst out laughing.

Brother Wasp laughed. He laughed until his side hurt him. He mashed his hand in his side to keep his side from hurting him. He rolled all around on the ground laughing. Every time he wanted to stop laughing, he thought about Brother Skeeter standing up there so proud of himself showing his little dry bone shank to show how big the potatoes in his Pa's field were, and he had to burst out laughing again.

When Brother Wasp was able to stop laughing, he had mashed his waist in little like the way you see it look now. This is the reason that Brother Wasp is so cross all the time. Brother Wasp wants to laugh like everybody else, but Brother Wasp is afraid that if he ever started

ain big mo'n uh dat dey'd be uh powerful po chance uh doing enny eatin, en e bus out laff.

Bus Was' laff. E laff tell e side hut um. E mash e han een e side fuh keep e side fuhm hut um. E roll all erbout on de groun duh laff. Ebby time e wa' stop laff, e study bout Buh Skeeter duh stan up dey so biggety duh show e leetle dry bone shank fuh show how big de tutter een e Pa fiel is, en e haf fuh bus out laff gen.

When Buh Was' bin able fuh stop laff, e had uh mash e wais een leetle lukka how yo shum stan now. En de cayjon fuh Buh Was' be so cross all de time. Buh Was does wa' laff lukka somebody, but Buh Was' faid say ef e ebber sta-a-t laff gen, e duh gwine bruk e self een two, so e haf fuh keep e self cross fuh keep fuhm laff.

laughing again that he will break himself in two. So, he has to keep himself cross to keep from laughing.

44-A6

BROTHER ALLIGATOR SEES TROUBLE

(HOW BROTHER ALLIGATOR GOT HIS MARKINGS)

1   Brother Alligator lived in the water where there was enough fish to eat, so he didn't have to work for a living, and he never met with trouble.

Brother Rabbit lived on the land and he met with plenty of trouble.

One time Brother Rabbit was rambling along the creek near Brother Alligator's house. Brother Rabbit met Brother Alligator sitting on the porch and he said, "Good morning, Brother Alligator. How are you and yours?"

Brother Alligator told him that he was getting along very well, and he asked Brother Rabbit how everyone was at his house.

44-A6

B'ALLEGETTER SEES TROUBLE

(HOW B'ALLEGETTER GIT E MA'KIN)

1   B'Allegetter lib een de watuh whey nuf uh fish dey fuh e eat, en e don' does haffuh wuk fuh e libbin, en e nebber meet up wid trouble.

Buh Rabbit lib on de lan en e meet up wid nuf uh trouble.

One time Buh Rabbit bin uh projec on de crick sho whey B'Allegetter house dey, and Buh Rabbit meet B'Allegetter duh set on e poach en e tell um say, "Good mawnin, B'Allegetter. How all uh younna?"

B'Allegetter tell um say all duh gittin on berry well, en e ax Buh Rabbit how all uh dem tuh him house.

5   Buh Rabbit tell um say dey

5   Brother Rabbit told him they were all making out but said, "There is too much trouble, Brother Alligator. Too much trouble."

Brother Alligator asked Brother Rabbit what trouble was and what it looked like.

Brother Rabbit said to Brother Alligator, "You have never seen trouble? I can show you trouble."

Brother Alligator told Brother Rabbit that he would like to see what trouble looked like. Brother Rabbit told him that if he would meet him in the broom sage field the next morning before the sun dried the dew off the grass, he would show him trouble.

The next morning as the sun was getting hot, Brother Alligator picked up his hat and started to leave the house. When Sister Alligator saw him going, she asked him where he was going. He told Sister Alligator that he was going to meet Brother Rabbit because he was going show him what trouble looked like.

10   Sister Alligator quarrelled with Brother Alligator and told

all duh mekkin out, "But summuch uh trouble, B'Allegetter. Summuch uh trouble."

B'Allegetter ax Buh Rabbit wuh duh trouble. How e stan?

Buh Rabbit ax B'Allegetter say, "B'Allegetter, yo ain nebber see trouble? Uh kin show you trouble."

B'Allegetter tell Buh Rabbit say him would uh like fuh see trouble fuh see how e stan. Buh Rabbit tell um say ef e would meet um een de broom sage fiel nex mawnin time de sun done dry de jew off de grass good, e would showed um trouble.

Nex mawnin time de sun bin git hot, B'Allegetter tek e hat en sta-a-t fuh lef de house. When S'Allegetter shum duh gwine, e ax um whey e duh gwine. E tell S'Allegetter say him duh gwine fuh meet Buh Rabbit fuh him fuh show um how trouble stan.

10   S'Allegetter qua'il en tell B'Allegetter ef him duh gwine, him duh gwine too. All de leetle allegetter yeddy dem duh qua'il en all uh dem holler say, "Ef younna duh gwine us duh gwine too. Ef younna duh gwine uh duh gwine

him if he was going, she was going too. All the little alligators heard them quarrelling and they all shouted, "If you're going, we're going too. If you're going we're going too."

They all made such a racket that Brother Alligator got tired of listening to them. He told them all to shut their mouths and come along then.

They all went across the marsh. By the time they got to the broom sage field to meet Brother Rabbit, he was sitting on top of a stump waiting for them.

They all told Brother Rabbit good morning, and the little alligators curtsied.

After Brother Rabbit told them all good morning, he asked Brother Alligator, "You all come to see trouble this morning, have you?"

15   Brother Alligator told him, yes, when he was leaving the house this morning they all begged to come. They all made such a racket that, to save his ears, he had to let them come too.

Brother Rabbit told them to stand out in the middle of the field,

too."

Dem all mek summuch uh racket tell B'Allegetter git tire fuh yeddy dem en e tell dem all fuh shet dem mout en come on den.

Dey all gone cross dem ma-a-sh en time dem git een de broom sage fiel, dem meet Buh Rabbit duh set puntop one stump duh wait fuh dem.

Dem all tell Buh Rabbit good mawnin, en de leetle allegetter mek dem curtschey.

At Buh Rabbit done tell dem all good mawnin, e ax B'Allegetter say, "Younna all come fuh see trouble dis mawnin, entty?"

15   B'Allegetter tell um say, yeh, when him bin uh gwine leff de house dis mawnin dem all baig fuh come, en dem all mek summuch uh racket tell, fuh sabe e yays, e haffuh le' dem come too.

Buh Rabbit tell dem stan out een de middle uh de fiel en tell dem fuh wait dey en him would go git trouble en bring um.

Buh Rabbit gone on de aig uh de fiel en e cut uh han uh broom sage en e put fire tuh um, en e run

29

then told them to wait there and he would go get trouble and bring it to them.

Brother Rabbit went to the edge of the field, cut a handful of broom sage, and set it on fire. Then he ran round and round so the fire caught around and around the field.

Directly, Sister Alligator saw the fire jumping up red and the smoke going up and she said, "Brother Alligator, what is that over there?" They lived in the river and the marsh and had never seen fire.

Brother Alligator told her that he didn't know what it was.

20   Sister Alligator said, "I think that is the trouble Brother Rabbit brought to show us."

All the little alligators jumped up and down shouting, "Aren't troubles pretty, Mom? Aren't trouble pretty?"

Soon the fire's heat closed in and the smoke got bad so they went to one side of the field. There they met the fire. They turned around and went to the other side. There they met the fire.

um roun en roun de fiel so de fire dey roun en roun de fiel.

Turrecly, S'Allegetter see de fire duh jumpin up red en de smoke duh gwine up, en e say, "B'Allegetter, wuh da yonder?" Dem lib een de ribber en de wet ma-a-sh, en ain nebber see fire.

B'Allegetter tell um say e dunno whu duh him.

20   S'Allegetter say, "Uh tink da's trouble Buh Rabbit duh bring fuh show we."

All de leetle allegetter jump up en down en holler, "Ain strubles pooty, ma? Ain strubles pooty?"

Turrecly, de fire hot git close, en de smoke git bad en dem tek out fuh one side de fiel. Dey meet de fire. Dey tun roun gone tarrer side. Dey meet de fire.

De fire git so close e feel luk e duh gwine bun dem.

Dey all shet dem yie en trowed dem head close tuh de groun en bus troo de fire en ain nebber stop tell B'Allegetter gone SPASHOW een de crick. Right behine um S'Allegetter SPASHOW een de crick. Al de

The fire's heat got so close they felt like it was going to burn them.

They all shut their eyes, lowered their heads close to the ground, and rushed through the fire and never stopped until Brother Alligator went SPASHOW in the creek. Right behind him Sister Alligator went SPASHOW in the creek. All the little alligators came shu shu shu shu shu shu in the creek.

25   As they were coming out of the field, Brother Rabbit was sitting on top of a stump and he shouted, "You've seen trouble now, Brother Alligator, you have seen trouble!"

The fire didn't get to the alligators' belly part, which was next to the ground and is still white. But all their backs burned until they were black and ridgy, just like you see them look today.

leetle allegetter come, shu, shu, shu, shu, shu, shu een de crick.

25   When dem duh comin out de fiel, Buh Rabbit bin uh set puntop one stump en e holler, "Yo done see trouble now B' Allegetter, you done see trouble!"

De fire ain bin git tuh de belly pa-a-t, wuh bin nex tuh de groun, en e yet white. But all dem back done bun tell e black en ridgy lukka how yo shum stan tell yet.

44-B1

44-B1

BROTHER RABBIT FOOLS BROTHER ELEPHANT AND BROTHER WHALE

BUH RABBIT FOOLS B'OLIFAUM* EN BUH WHALE

1   One time Brother Rabbit was out walking for pleasure and he met with Brother Elephant who was lying in his bed asleep. Brother Rabbit said, "Good morning, Brother Elephant."

Brother Elephant answered, "Good morning, Brother Rabbit."

Brother Rabbit said, "Gracious, Brother Elephant, you are surely a big man. You are bigger when you're lying down than when you're standing up."

Brother Elephant said, "Yes, Brother Rabbit, I am the biggest thing on earth."

5   Brother Rabbit said, "Brother Elephant, you know one thing?"

1   One time Buh Rabbit bin uh walk bout bin uh pledger e self en e meet up wid B'Olifaum duh leddown een e bed duh sleep. Buh Rabbit tell um say, "Good mawnin, B'Olifaum."

B'Olifaum gie um answer say, "Good mawnin, Buh Rabbit."

Buh Rabbit den say, "Greyshish, B'Olifaum, yo sho duh one able man. Yo big mo when yo duh leddown den when yo duh stan up."

B'Olifaum tell um say, "Yeh, Buh Rabbit, uh duh de bigges ting on de yut."

5   Buh Rabbit say,

*An Elephant to the Gullah people was an "Olifaum." Therefore, Buh (Brother) elephant was shortened to "B'Olifaum."

32

Brother Elephant said, "No, what is it?"

Brother Rabbit said, "Brother Elephant, as big as you are, and as little as I am, I bet I could pull you out of your bed."

Brother Elephant said, "What kind of talk is that, Brother Rabbit? Go away from here and leave me alone."

Brother Rabbit said to Brother Elephant, "Brother Elephant, if I were close enough to you for your size to scare me, it's true I couldn't pull you out of bed. But if you let me tie a rope to you and get back in the brush where I couldn't see you for your size to scare me, I'll bet you a hundred dollars I could pull you out of bed."

10   Brother Elephant said, "Go away from here, Brother Rabbit, leave me alone. I went to a dance last night and I danced the minute until dawn. I came here to lay down to catch some sleep and you have come here bothering me about pulling me out of my bed. You couldn't move one of my ears."

Brother Rabbit then told Brother Elephant that he was afraid

"B'Olifaum, yo know one ting?"

B'Olifaum tell um say, "No, wuh duh him?"

Buh Rabbit say, "B'Olifaum, big es yo is, en leetle es uh is, uh bet uh could pull yo out yo bed."

B'Olifaum say, "Wuh kine uh talk dat yo duh talk, Buh Rabbit? Gullong fuhm yuh, go lemme lone."

Buh Rabbit tell B'Olifaum say, "B'Olifaum, ef uh dey nigh'st yo fuh yo bigness fuh skayed me, uh couldn' pull yo out yo bed fuh true. But ef yo lemme tide rope tuh yo en get back een de bresh whey uh couldn' see yo fuh yo bigness fuh skayed me, uh bet uh hundud dolluh uh could pull yo out yo bed."

10   B'Olifaum say, "Do, Buh Rabbit, gullong fuhm yuh, go lemme lone. Uh bin tuh one dance last night en uh dance de minimit tell day clean. Uh come yuh fuh leddown fuh ketch some sleep en yo haffuh come yuh bodderation me bout pull me out muh bed. Yo couldn' moobe one uh muh yays."

Buh Rabbit den tell B'Olifaum say e's faid fuh bet um.

33

to bet with him.

Brother Elephant said again, "Go away and let me sleep."

Brother Rabbit pestered Brother Elephant and pestered Brother Elephant until, to get rid of him, Brother Elephant bet a hundred dollars that he couldn't pull him out of bed.

Brother Rabbit went along the river shore where he saw Brother Whale swimming in the river and he shouted, "Good morning, Brother Whale."

15   Brother Whale said, "Good morning, Brother Rabbit."

Brother Rabbit said, "Brother Whale, where have you been? I haven't seen you in a long time."

Brother Whale told him that, since he last saw him, he had been all the way around the world.

Brother Rabbit said, "Gracious, Brother Whale, you sure grew up to be one heck of a man."

Brother Whale told him, yes, he was the biggest thing in the river.

20   Then Brother Rabbit said,

B'Olifaum tell um gen say, "Fuh do fuh gullong en le' me sleep."

Buh Rabbit pester B'Olifaum, en e pester B'Olifaum tell, fuh git rid ur um, B'Olifaum bet um hundud dolluh say e couldn' pull um out e bed.

Buh Rabbit gone on de ribber sho whey e see Buh Whale duh swim duh ribber, en e holler say, "Good mawnin, Buh Whale."

15   Buh Wahle tell um say, "Good mawnin, Buh Rabbit."

Buh Rabbit say, "Buh Whale, whey yo bin? Uh ain see yo in long time."

Buh Wahle tell um say, sence e done shum las, e done bin clean roun de yut.

Buh Rabbit say, "Greyshish, Buh Whale, yo sho grow tuh be one abe man."

Buh Whale tell um say, yeh, him duh de bigges ting een de ribber.

20   Buh Rabbit den say, "Buh Whale, yo know one ting?"

Buh Wahle tell um say, "No,

"Brother Whale, you know one thing?"

Brother Whale said, "No, what's that?"

Brother Rabbit said, "Brother Whale, as little as I am, and as big as you are, I bet I could pull you out of the river."

Brother Whale said, "Go on, Brother Rabbit. What kind of talk are you talking? You couldn't move me in the river, let alone pull me out."

Brother Rabbit said, "Brother Whale, if I was there on the river shore to see your enormity when you were coming out of the water so your size would scare me, I truly couldn't pull you out of the river. But if you let me tie a rope to you so I can go behind the hill where I couldn't see you when you were coming out of water so your size would scare me, I'll bet you a hundred dollars I can pull you out of the river."

25   Brother Whale said that he wanted to see what Brother Rabbit was going to do, so he bet him the hundred dollars saying he couldn't pull him out of the river.

wuh duh him?"

Buh Rabbit say, "Buh Whale, leetle es uh is, en big es yo is, uh bet uh could uh pull yo out da ribber."

Buh Whale say, "Gullong, Buh Rabbit. Wha kine uh talk da yo duh talk? You couldn' moobe me een de ribber scusin fuh pull me out."

Buh Rabbit say, "Buh Whale, ef uh deddy on de ribber sho fuh see yo bigness when yo duh comin out de watuh fuh yo bigness fuh skayed me, uh couldn' pull yo out de ribber fuh true. But ef yo lemme tide one rope tuh yo so uh kin go back on de hill whey uh couldn' see yo when yo duh comin out de watuh fuh yo bigness fuh skayed me, uh bet yo hundud dolluh uh kin pull yo out da ribber."

25   Buh Whale say e bin uh wa' see wuh Buh Rabbit duh gwine do, so e bet um de hundud dolluh say e couldn' pull um out de ribber.

Buh Rabbit gone den en e git one long rope en e tek one een en e tide um tuh B'Olifaum. Den e tek tarrer een en e tide um tuh Buh Whale.

35

Then Brother Rabbit went to get a long rope. He took one end and tied it to Brother Elephant. Then he took the other and tied it to Brother Whale.

Brother Rabbit told each of them that when they felt the pulling begin, they must pull. Then he went to the middle of the rope and pulled so he was tugging on both ends at the same time.

Brother Elephant had lain down to sleep. He had forgotten about Brother Rabbit, but Brother Whale was waiting at the river to see what Brother Rabbit was going to do.

When Brother Whale felt Brother Rabbit pull, he jerked the rope hard.

30 The first thing Brother Elephant knew, he was jerked out of his bed and he went tumbling down the hill towards the river, unable to get on his feet.

When he did get on his feet, he wasn't able to stop himself from going toward the river. No matter how he hard he pulled, he just kept going toward the river.

If he hadn't seen two trees

Buh Rabbit tell dem all two say when dem feel him biggin pull, dem mus pull. Den e gone een de middle uh de rope en e tek um een all two e hans, en e pull fuhm all two eens one time.

B'Olifaum bin uh leddown een e bed bin uh sleep, en e ain bin ha Buh Rabbit een de back pa-a-t e head, but Buh Wahle bin uh wait duh ribber fuh see wuh Buh Rabbit duh gwine do.

When Buh Whale feel Buh Rabbit mek e pull, e mek uh big juk.

30 De fus ting B'Olifaum know e done juk out e bed en duh gwine sumbleset down de hill fuh de ribber, en e don' kin git on e foots.

When e does kin git on e foots e ain able fuh stop e'self fuh gwin e tuh de ribber. All B'Olifaum could uh pull, e dis keep duh gwine tuh de ribber.

Nummer e see two tree duh grow on de ribber sho' en e gone gone brace e'self gen dem tree, Buh Whale would uh pull um een de ribber en drownded um.

All Buh Whale pull e couldn' pull B'Olifaum en de tree,

growing on the river bank and braced himself against those trees, Brother Whale would have pulled him into the river and drowned him.

As much as Brother Whale pulled, he couldn't pull both Brother Elephant and the trees, so after a while, he got tired. He slackened up on the rope and Brother Elephant took up the slack, went back up the hill, and pulled Brother Whale completely out of the river.

If it hadn't been for the steep edge of the bank, Brother Elephant would have pulled him up on the high hill. Despite all of Brother Elephant's pulling, he couldn't pull Brother Whale over the lip of the bank.

35   Soon, Brother Elephant got tired and he slacked back on the rope. When Brother Whale made a jerk and went back into the river, he pulled Brother Elephant back to those same two trees again. If Brother Elephant hadn't braced himself against those trees again, Brother Whale would have pulled him into the river again and drowned him.

By and by, Brother Whale

en bum by, e git tire. E gie slack back on de rope en B'Olifaum tek de slack en gone back up on de hill en e pull Buh Whale clean out de ribber.

Nummer fuh de straight lif uh de bank, B'Olifaum would uh pull um on de high hill, but all B'Olifaum pull, e couldn' pull Buh Whale ober de straight lif uh de bank.

35   Turrecly B'Olifaum git tire en e gie slack back on de rope, en Buh Whale mek uh juk en e gone back een de ribber e pull B'Olifaum back tuh dem same two tree gen, en ef B'Olifaum ain gone brace e'self gen dem tree gen Buh Whale would uh pull um een de ribber en drownded um gen.

Bum by Buh Whale git tire en e gan gen duh try fuh pull B'Olifaum en de tree all two, en e gie slack back, en B'Olifaum tek de slack en e gone back up on de hill. When e gone back up on de hill Buh Rabbilt cut de rope.

When Buh Rabbit cut de rope, e gone whey B'Olifaum dey en e tell um say, "B'Olifaum, how yo tell me say uh couldn' pull yo out yo bed? Nummer uh ain bin wa' hut

got tired after trying to pull Brother
Elephant and both of the trees
again. As he gave slack back,
Brother Elephant took up the slack
and went back up the hill. When he
went back up the hill, Brother
Rabbit cut the rope.

After he cut the rope,
Brother Rabbit went over to
Brother Elephant and said,
"Brother Elephant, how come you
told me that I couldn't pull you out
of bed? If I hadn't wanted to avoid
hurting you, I would have pulled
you down the hill and thrown you
over my head into the river. But
then I would have had to pull you
out again."

Brother Elephant got very
angry and he said to Brother Rabbit, "You get out of here and leave
me alone."

Brother Rabbit said,
"Brother Elephant, you had best
pay me those hundred dollars that
you bet me before I jerk you up out
of that bed and throw you in the
river and drown you for sure."

40   Brother Elephant reached
into his pocket, pulled out a hundred dollars, and gave it to Brother
Rabbit.

yo, uh would uh pulled yo down da
hill en trowed yo ober muh head een
de ribber. But den uh would uh had
tuh pulled yo out gen."

B'Olifaum bin berry bex en
e tell Buh Rabbit say, "Gullong
fuhm yuh, go lemme lone."

Buh Rabbit say, "B'Olifaum,
yo bes pay me dem hundud dolluh
yo bet me fo' uh juk yo up out dat
bed en trowed yo een da ribber en
drownded yo fuh true."

40   B'Olifaum run e han een e
pawkit en pull out hundud dolluh
en gie um tuh Buh Rabbit.

Buh Rabbit den gone tuh de
ribber sho' whey Buh Whale duh
wait fuh see wuh Buh Rabbit haffuh
say fuh e self.

When Buh Rabbit see Buh
Whale e say, "Hey, Buh Whale, how
yo tell hut yo, uh'd uh pull'd yo on
de high hill, but den uh would uh
had tuh trowed yo back gen?"

Buh Whale say, "Greyshish,
Buh Rabbit, yo sho duh one able
leetle man. Ef uh bin able lukka
yo, en big lukka how uh is, uh could
moobe de yut."

Buh Whale run e han een e

Then Brother Rabbit went over to the river bank where Brother Whale was waiting to see what Brother Rabbit had to say for himself.

When Brother Rabbit saw Brother Whale, he said, "Hey, Brother Whale, how do you explain that, excepting that I didn't want to hurt you, I could've pulled you up onto the high hill, if I wouldn't have had to throw you back again?"

Brother Whale said, "Gracious, Brother Rabbit, you sure are a powerful little man. If I were as strong as you and as big as I am, I could move the world."

Brother Whale reached into his pocket and pulled out a hundred dollars and gave it to Brother Rabbit. Brother Rabbit grabbed that money and was gone with it.

pawkit en pull out hundud dolluh en gie um tuh Buh Rabbit, en Buh Rabbit tek de money en e gone wid um.

46-B4

46-B4

BROTHER FOX AND BROTHER ROOSTER

BUH FOX EN BUH ROOSTER

1   As the sun was setting one evening, Brother Rooster was kind of far from home when Brother Fox attacked him.

Brother Rooster ran and partly flew, but even at his top speed, Brother Fox was bound to catch him. Brother Rooster had to fly up into a tree to get away from him.

Brother Fox ran around and around, around and around underneath the branch where Brother Rooster was sitting, trying to make him so skittish that he would fall out of the tree so he could catch him.

Before Brother Rooster got skittish, he said to Brother Fox, "Brother Fox, why are you going through all of that to get a tough old rooster like me? A hen has made her nest in the hollow tree over there and she has raised a good

1   One ebenin gittin mos' tuh sun down Buh Rooster bin kine ub uh piece fuhm home when Buh Fox tek at um.

Buh Rooster run en pa-a-tly fly, but all e could do Buh Fox like tuh ketch um, en Buh Rooster hads fuh fly up een one tree fuh git way fuhm um.

Buh Fox run roun en roun, roun en roun, roun en roun on'neet de branch whey Buh Rooster duh set duh try fuh mek um giddish whey e would fall out de tree so e could ketch um.

Fo Buh Rooster git giddish e tell Buh Fox say, "Buh Fox, fuh whuf fuh yo do do all uh dat fuh git one tough ole rooster lukka me? One hen done tek nes een da holler tree ober dey en e done raise uh good gang un sizeubble chicken, en gang of sizeable chickens and they still use the same tree. They are in there now. Don't go up in front of the hole Brother Fox; they will see you and run out. Go up behind the tree and make them jump around in the hole and you'll shut them all up."

5 Sister Hound had taken the hole to raise her puppies in, and they had grown to a good size but they were still in there.

When Brother Fox heard about the hen and the gang of young chickens, he left Brother Rooster and went to the tree. He crept up to the tree almost on his belly. When he got to the tree he made one jump through the hole and landed right on top of Brother Hound and all his puppies.

All of them attacked Brother Fox at once, yelping, "YOW, WOW, WOW, LOUGH, LOUGH, YOW, YOW, LOUGH!" And they tore Brother Fox to bits.

When Brother Rooster heard the hounds were tearing up Brother Fox, he came down out of the tree and ran home cackling, "Goody-goody-GOODIE, goody-goody-GOODIE. Goody-goody-goody-GOODIE!"

dey yet nuse da same tree. Dem dey dey een dey now. Don' go up een front de holler Buh Fox, dem will see yo en run out. Go up behime de tree en mek up jump roun een de holler en yo'l shet up all."

5 Suh Houn had uh tek de holler fuh raise e puppy een, en dem had uh git tuh good size, but dey yet bin uh stid dey.

When Buh Fox yeddy bout de hen en de gang uh nyung chicken, e lef Buh Rooster en gone tuh de tree. E creep up tuh de tree mos' on e belly. When e git tuh de tree e mek one jump en gone een da hole right puntop Buh Houn en all e puppy.

All uh dem git on Buh Fox en sich uh hollerin! "YOW WOW WOW LOUGH LOUGH YOW YOW LOUGH!" En dey done tay up Buh Fox.

When Buh Rooster yeddy de houn duh tay up Buh Fox e come down out de tree en run home dis duh holler, "Goody-goody-GOODIE. Goody-goody-goody-GOODIE!"

BROTHER DEER AND BROTHER RABBIT RACE

1   Brother Deer and Brother Rabbit were talking one time and Brother Deer was bragging about how he could run. Brother Rabbit told him he couldn't run worth anything. He could outrun him.

Brother Deer said to Brother Rabbit, "Those short legs of yours aren't made for running. For every sixteen-foot jump I make, your short legs have to make many jumps to make one of mine."

Brother Rabbit told Brother Deer that, if they were to run in the road, Brother Deer would beat him for sure. He couldn't run in the road, but if Brother Deer would let him run in the brush beside the road, Brother Rabbit bet he could outrun him because he certainly could run in the brush.

BUH DEER EN BUH RABBIT RACE

1   Buh Deer en Buh Rabbit bin uh talk one time en Buh Deer bin uh brag how e could run. Buh Rabbit tell um say him couldn' run wut. Him could uh outrun um.

Buh Deer tell Buh Rabbit say, "Dey shawt laig uh younna ain stan fuh run. Ebby jumb mek duh sixteen foot, younna shawt laig haf fuh mek nuf uh jump fuh mek one uh mine."

Buh Rabbit tell Buh Deer say, ef dem was fuh run een de road, Buh Deer would beat um fuh true. Him can' run een de road but, ef e would le' um run een de bresh side de road, e bet e could outrun um, cay him sho kin run een de bresh.

Buh Deer tink say e wold uh wey Buh Rabbit down, so e tell um say e couldn' run no race les'n uh

Brother Deer thought he would wear Brother Rabbit down, so he told him he couldn't run a race unless it was a ten-mile race.

5 Brother Deer wanted to run right then, but Brother Rabbit told him he would have to go home to eat enough food to make him strong enough to run the race. So they decided to meet at sunrise the next morning to have the race.

Brother Rabbit went home and got all his family, and he got his brother and all of his brother's children and he put one to every mile post. Brother Rabbit himself went to the tenth mile post.

Next morning at sunrise Brother Deer came to the first mile post and he shouted, "Brother Rabbit, are you ready?" Brother Rabbit's brother was there in the brush beside the road and yelled, "Yes, let's go!"

Brother Deer made a jump and went down the road. He heard Brother Rabbit was running in the brush, quing quing quing, then suddenly he didn't hear him and he thought that he was so far past Brother Rabbit he was out of hearing.

tem-miles race.

5 Buh Deer does wa' run right den, but Buh Rabbit tell um say e would haf fuh go home eat nuf uh bittle fuh mek um strong fuh run da race. So dem mek out fuh meet nex sunrise nex mawnin en ha de race.

Buh Rabbit gone home en e git all e fambly, en e git e bredder en all e niece en e put one tuh ebby mile pos', en Buh Rabbit self gone tuh de ten miles pos'.

Nex mawnin sunrise Buh Deer come tuh de fus mile pos' en e holler, "Buh Rabbit, yuh ready?" Buh Rabbit bredder bin dey-dey een de bresh side de road, e holler, "Yeh, les go!"

Buh Deer mek e jump en e gon e down de road. E yeddy Buh Rabbit duh ru een de bresh, quing quing quing, den turrecly e ain yeddy um, en e tink say e done pas Buh Rabbit so fur e out uh yuhin.

When Buh Deer git mos' tuh de fus mile pos' e yeddy Buh Rabbit holler, "Come on, Buh Deer, uh diddy!" Den e yeddy um duh gwine, quing quing quing quing, tru de bresh. Buh Deer lay e self tuh de

When Brother Deer got almost to the first mile post, he heard Brother Rabbit shout, "Come on, Brother Deer, I'm up here!" Then he heard him going quing quing quing quing through the brush. Brother Deer dug into the ground. But as hard as he ran, when he was coming to the two mile post, he heard Brother Rabbit shout, "What are you doing, Brother Deer? Why don't you run?" Then he heard Brother Rabbit going quing quing quing quing through the brush.

10   Every mile post Brother Deer got to, Brother Rabbit was there before him. When he got to the last mile post, he met Brother Rabbit sitting down by the side of the road, waiting for him.

Brother Rabbit said, "Brother Deer, I thought you said you could run. You can't run worth a darn. Brother Terrapin could outrun you."

Brother Deer was angry that Brother Rabbit beat him. He blurted, "That short-legged thing! He can't even run. He has to crawl."

Brother Rabbit told Brother groun, but all e could run when e duh coming tuh de two mile pos' e yeddy Buh Rabbit holler, "Wuh yo duh do, Buh Deer, mek yo don't run?" Den e yeddy Buh Rabbit duh gwin quing quing quing quin tru de bresh.

10   Ebby mile pos' Buh Deer git tuh Buh Rabbit dey-dey befo um, en when e git tuh de las mile pos' e meet Buh Rabbit duh set down side de road duh wait fuh um.

Buh Rabbit say, "Buh Deer, uh taught say yo say yo could uh run. Yo ca' run wut. Buh Cooter could outrun yo."

Buh Deer bin bex fuh Buh Rabbit beat um en e say, "Da shawt laig ting! E ca' much es run, e haf fuh crawl."

Buh Rabbit tell Buh Deer say e ain mean fuh Buh Cooter fuh run on de lan, Buh Cooter fuh swim duh ribber en Buh Deer fuh run de ribber road, en e bet um e would uh beat um.

Buh Deer say Buh Cooter ain fuh beatin' um, e dunk'yer how e do, en dem mek plan fuh ha de race nex day, en Buh Deer say e would haf fuh be nedder ten-miles race.

Deer that he didn't mean for Brother Terrapin to run on land. Brother Terrapin would swim in the river while Brother Deer ran on the river road, and he bet him that Brother Terrapin could beat him.

Brother Deer bragged that Brother Terrapin couldn't beat him, regardless of how he raced him. So they made plans to have the race the next day, and Brother Deer said it would have to be another ten-mile race.

15   Brother Rabbit got all of Brother Terrapin's family and he put one of them to every mile. He set up Brother Terrapin himself to do the last mile.

The next morning, when Brother Deer came to the first mile post, he met one of the terrapins sitting on top of a log that was by the first mile post. Brother Deer asked him if he was ready and he told him that, yes, he was ready.

Then Brother Deer said, "Let's go." And he took off running. When Brother Deer shouted, "Let's go," Brother Terrapin slipped off the log, poo-ju-loonk, into the river.

15   Buh Rabbit git all uh Buh Cooter fambly en e put one ur dem to ebby mile, en Buh Cooter self e put to de las mile.

Nex mawnin when Buh Deer come tuh de fus mile pos' e meet one uh de cooter duh set puntop one log wuh dey tuh de fus mile pos'. Buh Deer ax um is e ready, en Buh Cooter tell um say, yeh, e ready.

Buh Deer den say, "Les we go." En e tek out run. When Buh Deer holler, "Les go," Buh Tarrapin gone off de lo-o-g, poo-ju-loonk, een de ribber.

Buh Deer tink say e so sho fuh beat Buh Cooter tell e nebber run fas. When e git tuh de fus mile pos' Buh Cooter dey dey duh set puntop one long, e holler say, "Uh bin uh wait fuh yo, Buh Deer." Poo-ju-loonk, e gone een de ribber.

Buh Deer stretch e self but when e git tuh de nex mile Buh Cooter dey dey duh wait fuh um. Poo-ju-loonk, e gone een de ribber.

20   All Buh Deer could run e meet Buh Cooter ebby mile duh wait fuh um. When e git tuh de las mile, Buh Cooter tell um, "Buh

47

Brother Deer was so sure he would beat Brother Terrapin that he never ran fast. When he got to the first mile post, Brother Terrapin was sitting there on top of a log. He shouted, "I've been waiting for you, Brother Deer." Poo-ju-loonk, he slid into the river.

Brother Deer stretched himself but when he got to the next mile, Brother Terrapin was there waiting for him. Poo-ju-loonk, he dropped into the river.

20   As fast as Brother Deer could run, Brother Terrapin was waiting for him after every mile. When he got to the last mile, Brother Terrapin taunted him some more, "Brother Deer, what have you been doing? I've been waiting for you on top of this log for such a long time that my shell has dried out and started to crack up."

Brother Deer wasn't satisfied. He thought Brother Terrapin was fooling him. Brother Deer said he had to run the race over again and he wanted to run it immediately.

Brother Rabbit said to Brother Deer, "Brother Deer, Brother Terrapin swam so hard that

Deer, wuh yo bin uh do? Uh wait yuh fuh yo puntop dis log so long time tell muh shell done dry tell e fay crack up."

Buh Deer ain bin satify, e tink say Buh Rabbit had uh jook um en e say e would hads fuh ha run da race ober gen, en e wa' run um right den.

Buh Rabbit tell Buh Deer say, "Buh Deer, Buh Cooter swim so ha-a-d tell e done. Yo ain run wut en yo ain tired one tall. Buh Cooter couldn' run da race gen tell tuhmorrer. E haf fuh res."

Buh Deer tek up buh Cooter en e cut tree ma-a-k puntop Buh Cooter bottom shell. One de ma-a-k dey from e neck tuh e tail, de yedder dey crost e bottom shell fuhm one hine laig tuh tarrer, en de front one fuhm one front laig tuh tarrer.

Buh Deer put Buh Cooter down en tell um say e fuh meet um tuh de fus mile sunrise nex mawnin, en e gone on.

25   Da ebenin Buh Rabbit tek all uh Buh Cooter fambly en e mak de same self ma-a-k on ebby one wuh Buh Deer had uh mek on Buh

he's spent. You didn't run very hard and you're not tired at all. Brother Terrapin couldn't run the race again until tomorrow. He has to rest."

Brother Deer turned Brother Terrapin over and he cut three marks into Brother Terrapin's bottom shell. One of the marks was from his neck to his tail, the other was across his bottom shell from one hind leg to the other, and the front one ran from one front leg to the other.

Brother Deer set Brother Terrapin down. He told him to meet him at the first mile at sunrise the next morning and he left.

25   That evening Brother Rabbit called all of the terrapins to meet at the mile post and wait for him. He tipped each of them up and looked at the bottom of their shells. He put the same marks on each one, and he had to admit each looked like Brother Terrapin himself.

They had the race and every mile Brother Deer met Brother Terrapin there sitting on a log shouting, "Come on, Brother Deer. Come on, Brother Deer." Poo-ju-loonk, he scudded into the river.

Cooter self, den e tek en put one tuh ebby mile pos' gen. Next mawnin when Buh Deer come e meet Buh Cooter uh de fus mile pos' duh wait fuh um. E tek um up en look tuh de bottom shell en e see de same self ma-a-k e had uh put on, en e hads fuh bleebe say duh Buh Cooter self.

Dem mek de race en ebby mile Buh Deer meet Buh Cooter dey puntop one lo-o-g duh holler, "Come on, Buh Deer, come on Buh Deer." Poo-ju-loonk, e gone een de ribber.

When Buh Deer git tuh de ten mile pos' e meet Buh Cooter duh wait fuh um, e tek up Buh Cooter en look puntop e bottom shell en e see de berry same self ma-a-k e had uh mek e self en e hads fuh say Buh Cooter beat um.

Den ma-a-k wuh Buh Rabbit put on Buh Cooter ain nebber come out. Tell yet Buh Cooter ha dem same m-a-kin on e bottom shell.

When Brother Deer got to
the ten mile post, there was Brother
Terrapin waiting for him. He
tipped up Brother Terrapin and
looked at his bottom shell. He saw
the very same mark he had made
himself and had to admit that
Brother Terrapin had beaten him.

The marks Brother Rabbit
put on the terrapins never came
out. Brother Terrapin has had the
very same markings on the bottom
of his shell to the present day.

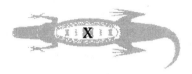

HE MIGHT OVERRUN THE LAW

E MIGHT OBER RUN DE LAW

1   Brother Turkey was picking up acorns underneath an oak tree when Brother Fox burst out of the brush and made Brother Turkey fly up in the tree to save himself.

Brother Fox pretended he was eating an acorn. He chomped his mouth and said, "Brother Turkey, this is the sweetest acorn I ever tasted in my life. You ought to come down and taste some."

Brother Turkey told him that he didn't want anymore, he had all he wanted.

Brother Fox then said to Brother Turkey, "Brother Turkey, you haven't heard about the new law they passed?"

5   Brother Turkey told him he hadn't heard about a law. "What law was that?"

1   Buh Tukrey bin uh pick akon on'neet one oak tree when Buh Fox bus out de bresh en mek Buh Tukrey fly up een de tree sabe e'self.

Buh Fox mek luk e duh eat de akon, en e chomp e mout en e say, "Buh Tukrey, dis yuh duh de sweetes akon uh ebber tase een muh life. Yo bes come down tase some."

Buh Tukrey tell um say e ain bin wa' no mo, e done ha all e doe's wa'.

Buh Fox den tell Buh Tukrey say, "Buh Tukrey, yo ain yeddy bout de new law done pas?"

5   Buh Tukrey tell um say no e ain no yeddy bout no law. "Wuh law dat?"

Buh Fox tell um, "Yeh, one law done pas say all de creeter fur be

Brother Fox said, "Yes, a law was passed that says that all the creatures must be friends. Fox isn't to bother Fowl, Hound isn't to bother Fox, they're all supposed to live together. Why don't you come on down here, Brother Turkey, and share these sweet acorns with me?"

Brother Turkey wouldn't come down. Brother Fox kept begging him to come down but Brother Turkey wouldn't come.

After a while, they heard some hounds coming. They kept getting closer and closer. Soon Brother Fox said, "I'll just be going, Brother Turkey."

Brother Turkey asked him, "What are you leaving for? Didn't you tell me that a law was passed that said all the creatures were supposed to live together?"

10   Brother Fox said, "Yes, Brother Turkey, that law was truly passed, but those long-legged devils run so fast, they might overrun the law!"

fren. Fox ain fuh bodder Fowl, Houn ain fuh bodder Fox, all fuh lib tu'gedder. Mek yo do' come down, Buh Tukrey, en shay dis yuh sweet akon wid me?"

Buh Tukrey wouldn' come down, en Buh Fox keep duh baig am fuh come down, but Buh Tukrey wouldn' come.

Turrecly, dem yeddy some houns duh comin, en dem duh keep duh gittin closter en turrecly Buh Fox say, "Uh jus be gwine, Buh Tukrey."

Buh Tukrey ax um say, "Fuh whuf fuh yo duh gwine, entty yo tell me say one law done pas say all de creetr fur lib tu'gedder?"

10   Buh Fox say, "Yeh, Buh Tukrey, da law done pas fuh true, but dem long-laig debbil run so fas, dem might ober run de law!"

46-A6

IS A LONG BILL A GOOD THING?

1   Brother Crane was a fisherman, and when he went fishing he caught plenty of fish.

He and Brother Rabbit were talking one day and Brother Crane said to Brother Rabbit, "Brother Rabbit, let's put on a dance."

Brother Rabbit told him, yes, he would really like to have a dance, but where would they get the money to buy the things to put on a dance with?

Brother Crane told him that he would go fishing and Brother Rabbit could take the fish he caught and sell them to buy things for the dance.

5   Brother Crane went into the river and caught plenty of fish to give to Brother Rabbit to sell to get liquor, food, and things for the

46-A6

LONG BILL DUH GOOD TING?

1   Buh Crane duh one fishermun, en when e does go fishnin e does ketch nuf fish.

Him en Buh Rabbit bin uh talk one day, en Buh Crane tell Buh Rabbit say, "Buh Rabbit, les we gie one dance."

*Buh Rabbit tell um say yeh, e would likes fuh gie one dance fuh true, but whey dem duh gwine git de money fuh buy ting fuh gie de dance wid?

Buh Crane tell um say him would go fishnin en Buh Rabbit fuh tek de fish e ketch e sell um en buy ting fuh de dance.

5   Buh Crane gone een de ribber en e ketch nuf uh fish en e gie um tuh Buh Rabbit fuh sell en

*Paragraphs 3 & 4 were combined in original typescript.

dance. Then he told him to buy cake and things, as well as a five-gallon jug of liquor, and he told him not to buy cups. "If you have cups the people are going to drink too much of the liquor, but if they have to lift up the jug, they won't drink as much."

Brother Rabbit took the fish and sold them to get all that he needed for the dance, including the five-gallon jug of liquor.

They took the jug and put it behind the door, and when the people came, Brother Crane told them he was going to call the figure and Brother Rabbit was going to play the fiddle.

Brother Crane ran behind the door and shoved his long bill down into the jug and took a big drink. Then he came out to call the figure, and every time he swung, he swung behind the door and shoved his bill down to get another drink.

When Brother Rabbit had played one dance, he went behind the door to get a drink but the jug was too heavy for him to lift. He tried to run his tongue down in the jug but it was too short to get to the liquor. He tried every possible way

git likker, en bittle, en ting fuh de dance. En e tell um say e fuh buy cake en ting, en e fuh buy uh five-gallon jug uh likker, en e tell um gen say e ain fuh buy no cup. "Ef yo ha cup de people duh gwine drink tummuck uh de likker, but ef dey haffuh hi'se de jug dey ain gwine drink summuch."

Buh Rabbit tek de fish en sell um en git all wuh e does need fuh de dance, en e git one five-gallon jug uh likker.

Dem tek de jug en put um behime de do', en when de people come Buh Crane tell um say him duh gwine call de figger en Buh Rabbit duh gwine play de fiddle.

Buh Crane run behime de do' en shub e long bill down een de jug en e tek uh big drink. Den e come out call de figger, en ebby time e swing e swing behime de do' en shub e bill down en e git nedder drink.

When Buh Rabbit done play one dance, e gone behime de do' fuh git one drink but de jug bin too hebby fuh him lif. E try fuh run e tongue down een de jug, but e bin too shawt fuh meet de likker. Ebby way e try e ain bin able fuh git none.

but wasn't able to get any.

10   He went back, picked up his fiddle and played another tune. While he played he sang: "Plenty of trouble and I tried so hard. I couldn't get any and I wanted some bad."

Nobody except Brother Crane knew what Brother Rabbit was singing about.

Every time Brother Crane swung, he went behind the door and took a drink. Soon he ran his bill down into the jug and hit the bottom of the jug. It was bone dry. He came back, took up the dance and he sang, "All done gone, it's all bone dry. Lift it now if you only try. A long bill is a good thing to suck it dry."

Brother Rabbit knew that Brother Crane had taken advantage of him while he was making music for all of them, and he was angry. He got even more angry because, while he was playing the fiddle, Brother Crane danced every dance with Brother Rabbit's girlfriend. Brother Rabbit played the fiddle and sang:

"All done gone. All bone

10   E gone out, tek e fiddle en play nedder chune. While e duh play e duh sing: "Nuf uh trouble en uh try so ha-a-d. Uh couldn' git none en uh wa' some bad."

No body nummer Buh Crane know wuh Buh Rabbit duh sing bout.

Ebby time Buh Crane swing, e gone behime de doe en a tek uh drink. Turrecly e run e bill down een de jug en e hit de bottom en e meet de jug done dry. E come out e tek up de dance en e sing "All done gone, e all done dry, lif um now ef yo ondly try, long bill duh good ting fuh mek um dry."

Buh Rabbit know say Buh Crane had uh tek exwansus tur um while e duh mek music fuh all uh dem, en e git bex. E mo'ober bex gen, cay while e duh play de fiddle Buh Crane dance ebby dance wid Buh Rabbit gal. Buh Rabbit duh play duh fiddle en duh sing.

"All done gone, all done dry, fo sun up, uh gwine mek yo cry."

15   Turrecly Buh Crane lef de dance en e gone outside en led down on de groun en gone sleep. Buh Rabbit git someone fuh play de fiddle fuh dem fuh dance by, en e

57

dry. Before the dawn, I m going to make you cry."

15   Brother Crane left the dance soon after, went outside, laid down on the ground and went to sleep. Brother Rabbit got someone to play the fiddle for everyone to dance by and he danced every dance with the girl.

It was fully daylight before the dance broke up. Brother Rabbit was with the girl and was taking her home. When they were leaving the house, Brother Crane lifted up his head and he said, "Are you going home now, sure enough?"

Brother Rabbit said, "Yes, Brother Crane, you long-mouthed devil, you're the one who got all the liquor, but I'm the one who got the girl."

dance ebby dance wid de gal.

E bin day clean fo de dance bruk up, en Buh Rabbit bin ha de gal duh tekkin um home. When dem duh leffin de house, Buh Crane lif up e haid en e say, "Younna duh gwine home now, entty?"

Buh Rabbit tell um say, "Yeh, Buh Crane, yo long-mout debbil yo de one git all de likker, but I de one git de gal."

46-B1

46-B1

DON'T TRUST BROTHER RATTLESNAKE'S WORD

DON' TRUS BUH RATTLESNEAK WUD

1   Brother Rattlesnake was going through the woods one time when a log fell on top of him and pinned him to the ground. As much as he could coil and twist, he couldn't get out from underneath the log.

He was stuck there a long time when Brother Wolf happened to come by. As soon as Brother Rattlesnake saw him, he shouted, "Brother Wolf, come lift this log from on top of me so I can get out!"

Brother Wolf said to Brother Rattlesnake, "No, Brother Rattlesnake, uh umh. If I lift that log, you are going to charm me. I am not going to get close enough to you for you to be able to charm me."

Brother Rattlesnake begged Brother Wolf, "Please, Brother Wolf, come lift this log off of me.

1   Buh Rattlesneak bin uh gwine troo de wood one time, en one log fall puntop um en fasen um tuh de groun. All e could quile en twis e could'n git fuhm on'neet da log.

E bin fasen dey long time when Buh Wolf happen tuh come by. Time Buh Rattlesneak shum, e holler, "Do, Buh Wolf, come lif dis yuh log fuhm puntop me so uh kin git out."

Buh Wolf tell Buh Rattlesneak say, "No, Buh Rattlesneak, uh umh. Ef uh lif da log yo duh gwine cha-a-am me. Uh ain duh gwine git close nuf tuh yo fuh yo fuh cha-a-am me."

Buh Rattlesneak baig Buh Wolf, "Do, Buh Wolf, come lif dis yuh log fuhm puntop me. E duh

It is hurting my back very badly."
He promised Brother Wolf faithfully
that he wouldn't charm him.

5   Brother Wolf went over to
him and lifted the log off Brother
Rattlesnake. As soon as Brother
Rattlesnake came out from under
the log, he looked Brother Wolf
right in the eye.

    Brother Wolf couldn't turn
his eye away from Brother
Rattlesnake's eye and soon Brother
Wolf couldn't move. He was standing there trembling and trying to
hold himself back from getting
closer to Brother Rattlesnake.

    Brother Rabbit just happened
to come along, and Brother Wolf had
enough sense left to call him.

    Brother Rabbit went over to
him, and Brother Wolf said, "I
came this way this morning and
met Brother Rattlesnake pinned
down with a log that had fallen on
top of him. He begged me to lift
the log so he could come out.

    "I said to him, 'Uh umh, if I
get that close to you, you are going
to charm me.' He promised me
faithfully that if I let him loose he
wouldn't charm me."

hut muh back bad." E promise
Buh Wolf faitful say e would'n cha-
a-am um.

5   Buh Wolf gone dey, e lif de
log fuhm puntop Buh Rattlesneak.
Time Buh Rattlesneak come fuhm
on'neet de log, e look Buh Wolf
right een e yie.

    Buh Wolf could'n tun e yie
fuhm Buh Rattlesneak yie, en
turrecly Buh Wolf could'n moobe.
E duh stan dey duh trimble en duh
try fuh hole e self fuhm go tuh Buh
Rattlesneak.

    Happen so Buh Rabbit come
long, en Buh Wolf ha nuf sense lef
fuh call Buh Rabbit.

    Buh Rabbit gone tur um, en
Buh Wolf tell um say, "Uh come dis
way dis mawnin en meet Buh
Rattlesneak fasen down wid one log
wuh had uh fall puntop um. E baig
me fuh lif de log so e could come
out.

    "Uh tell um say, 'Uh umh,
ef uh git da close tuh yo, yo duh
gwine cha-a-am me.' E promise me
faitful say ef uh loose um e would'n
cha-a-am me."

10   Buh Rabbit tell Buh
Rattlesneak say, "Buh Rattlesneak,

10   Brother Rabbit said to Brother Rattlesnake, "Brother Rattlesnake, you have never been underneath that log. You couldn't get underneath that log to save your life."

Brother Rattlesnake said he certainly had been underneath that log.

Brother Rabbit said, "Brother Rattlesnake, you've never been underneath that log. The only way I'll believe you were there is for you to go back underneath it."

He told Brother Wolf to lift up the log again. By the time he lifted up the log, Brother Rattlesnake had gone underneath it. At the same time he went underneath it, Brother Rabbit yelled, "Turn it loose, Brother Wolf! Turn it loose!"

Brother Wolf let it go and it pinned Brother Rattlesnake to the ground again. Brother Rattlesnake was so mad he shook his rattle and he twisted and he coiled, trying to get out, but he couldn't loose himself.

15   As Brother Rabbit and Brother Wolf ambled off, Brother Rabbit said to Brother Wolf, "Brother Wolf, don't go near Brother Rattlesnake, and don't you ever trust Brother Rattlesnake's word."

yo ain nebber bin on'neet da log. Yo could'n git on'neet da log fuh sabe yo life."

Buh Rattlesneak say e sho is bin on'neet da log.

Buh Rabbit say, "Buh Rattelsneak, yo nebber bin on'neet da log. De ondly way uh'l bleebe yo bin dey is fuh yo fuh go back on'neet um."

E tell Buh Wolf fuh lif up de log gen. Time e lif up de log Buh Rattlesneak gone 'neet um. Time e gone on'neet um, Buh Rabbit holler say, "Tun um loose Buh Wolf! Tun um loose!"

Buh Wolf tun um loose en e fasen Buh Rattlesneak tuh de groun gen. Buh Rattlesneak bin so mad e sing e rattle en duh twis en quile fuh come out, but e could'n loose e self.

15   Buh Rabbit en Buh Wolf gone off, en Buh Rabbit tell Buh Wolf say, "Buh Wolf, don' go nigh'st Buh Rattlesneak, en don' yo nebber trus Buh Rattlesneak wud."

61

45-A3

BROTHER BLACKSNAKE GETS CAUGHT

1   Brother Blacksnake went into Brother Rabbit's yard one time, caught one of Brother Rabbit's children, and ate him. Brother Rabbit got very angry. He went to get some boards to make a tight fence all the way around the yard and told the children not to go out of the yard at all.

One of the boards that was close to the ground had a knot hole in it. Every day Brother Blacksnake came to peek his eye through the hole to see if one of Brother Rabbit's children were close to the hole. But he wouldn't trust his luck to come inside. He was afraid that Brother Rabbit might pen him up in there.

Brother Rabbit knew that he* was going to come in and trust his

Brother Blacksnake, his adversary.

45-A3

BUH BLACK SNEAK GIT KETCH

1   Buh Black Sneak gone een Buh Rabbit ya-a-d one time en ketch one uh Buh Rabbit chillun en eat um, en dat bex Buh Rabbit tummuch en e gone git some boad en mek tight fench roun en roun de ya-a-d, en tell de chillun dem say e ain none uh dem fuh go out da ya-a-d none tall.

One uh de boad wuh low tuh dc groun bin ha one knots hole een um, en ebby day Buh Black Sneak does come peep e yie troo de hole fuh see ef one uh Buh Rabbit chillun dey close de hole. But e wouldn' trus e luck fuh come een. E faid say Buh Rabbit might uh pen um up een dey.

Buh Rabbit know say e duh gwine trus e luck fuh come een one dese days, so e does set all kine ub uh trap fuh ketch Buh Black Sneak, but Buh Black Sneak too luck one of these days, so he set all kinds of traps to catch Brother Blacksnake. But Brother Blacksnake was too sharp to go into any of the traps.

Brother Rabbit went to where Sister Hen had a nest. When Sister Hen was off of the nest, Brother Rabbit stole two of the eggs. He set one of the eggs outside of the fence by the knot hole. He set the other egg inside the fence by the knot hole.

5   Soon Brother Blacksnake came along and saw the egg there on the ground. He said, "Eh, eh, someone left an egg here." Then, he swallowed the egg, looked through the knot hole, and saw the other egg there. He said, "Eh, eh, there is another egg."

He looked all around, saw no one, ran his head through the fence, and swallowed the egg.

After he had swallowed both of the eggs, they each made a lump in his body. One was on the outside of the fence and the other was on the inside. Brother Blacksnake could go neither in nor out.

Brother Rabbit was watching

sha-a-p fuh go een none uh de trap.

Buh Rabbit gone whey Suh Hen bin ha one nes', en when Suh Hen dey off de nes', Buh Rabbit teef two de aig. E set one de aig outside de fench by de knots hole. E set de yedder aig eenside de fench by de knots hole.

5   Turrecly Buh Black Sneak come see de aig dey-dey on de groun, e say, "Eh eh, someone done lef one aig yuh." En e tun een en swallered de aig. E look troo de knots hole en e see tarrer aig dey-dey. E say, "Eh eh, nedder aig dey-dey gen."

E look all erbout, e ain see no one, en e run e head troo de fench en swallered da aig.

At e done swallered all two de aig, e ha knots wuh de aig mek een um. One dey on de outside de fench en de tarrer dey eenside, en Buh Black Sneak couldn' come een needer go out.

Buh Rabbit bin uh watch um, en when e see e done ketch e bring all e fambly en stan dem right up een Buh Black Sneak face, en e say, "Mek you don' come een, Buh Black Sneak, all muh chillun dey him. When he saw he'd caught his quarry, he brought all of his family and stood them right up in Brother Blacksnake's face. He said, "Why don't you come in, Brother Black-snake? All of my children are right here. Come in and get one of the children. How did you get caught in the trap if you're so smart?"

All of this made Brother Blacksnake so mad that he twisted and he coiled, twisted and coiled, until the sharp edge of the knot hole cut him almost in two. He died right there and he never got any of Brother Rabbit's children.

dey right yuh. Come in an git one uh de chillun. How yo too sha-a-p fuh go een trap, Buh Black Sneak?"

All dat mek Buh Black Sneak so mad tell e twis en e quile; twis en e quile, tell de sha-a-p aidge de knots hole cut um mos' een two, en e dead right dey en e ain nebber git none uh Buh Rabbit chillun.

45-B1

BROTHER RABBIT WANTS MORE KNOWLEDGE

1   Brother Rabbit schemed too much and he was so smart that he could fool all the other creatures except for Brother Partridge. Every time Brother Rabbit tried to scheme on Brother Partridge, Brother Partridge got the best of Brother Rabbit.

Brother Rabbit wanted to be the smartest thing in the world, and he schemed to try to fool Father. He should have known the Father couldn't be fooled.

He went to Father. After he displayed the proper manners, Father asked him what he wanted. Brother Rabbit said to Father, "Please, sir, I want more knowledge."

Father told Brother Rabbit that he couldn't give him his knowledge right then, but if he would do

45-B1

BUH RABBIT WATN MO ACKNOWLEDGE

1   Buh Rabbit bin schemey tummuch en e bin sma-a-t tell e could er fool all de tarrer creeter scusin tuh Buh Pa-a-tridge, en ebby time Buh Rabbit try e schemey puntop Buh Pa-a-tridge, Buh Pa-a-tridge does git de bes' uh Buh Rabbit.

Buh Rabbit does wa' be de sma-a-tes ting een de wul, en e tek e schemey en try fuh fool Farrer. E ought tuh bin know say Farrer en duh gwine tek e schemey.

E gone tuh Farrer. At e done mek e mannus, Farrer ax um say, wuh e does wa'. Buh Rabbit tell Farrer say, "Please, suh, uh does wa' mo acknowledge."

Farrer tell Buh Rabbit say e couldn' gie um e acknowledge right den, but if e would do dis dizactly

65

exactly what he was going to tell him to do, he would get his knowledge.

5   Father told Brother Rabbit to bring him the biggest blacksnake he could find, bring him a wild bee's nest, and bring him one alligator's tusk.

Brother Blacksnake catches rabbits and eats them, and Brother Rabbit was afraid of Brother Blacksnake.

As for Brother Bee, Brother Rabbit wasn't so scared of Brother Bee, but when he goes by the bee tree and tries to lick some of the honey that might drip down the tree, Brother Bee stings him on the nose.

Brother Alligator and Brother Rabbit were good friends at one time, but after Brother Rabbit set Brother Alligator's marsh on fire and almost burned up Brother Alligator and all his family, Brother Alligator had a big grudge against Brother Rabbit and he tries to catch him to kill him.

Brother Rabbit went home to think about the thing. Directly he went into the woods and cut himself a long pole. He put the

lukka how e duh gwine tell um fuh do, e would git e acknowledge.

5   Farrer tell Buh Rabbit say e fuh bring um de bigges blacksneak e kin fine, e fuh bring um one nes' uh wile bee, en e fuh bring um one allegetter tursh.

Buh Black Sneak does catch Buh Rabbit en eat um, en Buh Rabbit faid uh Buh Black Sneak.

As fuh Buh Bee, Buh Rabbit ain say so skayed uh Buh Bee, but when Buh Rabbit does go by de bee tree en try fuh leek some uh de honey wuh might uh drap down out de tree, Buh Bee does come sting um on e nose.

B'Allegetter en Buh Rabbit bin good frens one time, but at Buh Rabbit set B'Allegetter ma-a-sh fire en like fuh bun up B'Allegetter en all e fambly, B'Allegetter bin ha big tippety gin Buh Rabbit en e does try fuh ketch um fuh kill um.

Buh Rabbit gone home en e study puntop dat ting. Turrecly e gone een de wood en cut e self one long pole. E put de ting on e shoulder en e walk, en e walk, tell e meet up wid one big ole black sneak duh leddown duh sun e self.

thing on his shoulder and he walled and he walked until he met up with a big old blacksnake that was lying down sunning himself.

10   He said, "Good morning, Brother Blacksnake."

Brother Blacksnake said, "Good morning, Brother Rabbit."

Brother Rabbit said, "Brother Blacksnake, you certainly have grown into a big man."

Brother Blacksnake said, "Yes, Brother Rabbit, I've been here a long time. It was I who ate your granddaddy."

Brother Rabbit then said, "Gracious, Brother Blacksnake, you certainly have grown to be a big man. I'll bet you're almost as long as this pole I have."

15   Brother Blacksnake said to Brother Rabbit, "Get out of here, Brother Rabbit, that pole isn't nearly as long as I am."

Brother Rabbit said, "I don't know, Brother Blacksnake. This is a very long pole. Let's measure."

Brother Blacksnake said, "If you want to measure, go ahead and

10   E tell um say, "Good mawnin, Buh Black Sneak."

Buh Black Sneak tell um say, "Good mawnin, Buh Rabbit."

Buh Rabbit say, "Buh Black Sneak, yo sho duh grow to be one able man."

Buh Black Sneak tell um say, "Yeh, Buh Rabbit, uh bin yuh long time, duh me eat yo grandaddy."

Buh Rabbit den say, "Greyshish, Buh Black Sneak, yo sho grow tuh be uh able man. Uh bet yo mos' long lukka dis yuh pole uh got."

15   Buh Black Sneak tell Buh Rabbit say, "Gullong, Buh Rabbit, da pole ain nuttin long lukka me."

Buh Rabbit say, "Uh dunno, Buh Black Sneak. Dis yuh duh one berry long pole. Les we medjur."

Buh Black Sneak tell Buh Rabbit say, "Ef yo wa' medjur, gullong medjur. Uh done tell yo say da pole ain nuttin long lukka me."

Buh Rabbit put de ple down long side Buh Black Sneak, en Buh Black Sneak lack nuf fuh be long ez measure. I've already told you, that pole isn't nearly as long as I am."

Brother Rabbit put the pole down along side Brother Blacksnake and Brother Blacksnake wasn't as long as the pole.

Brother Rabbit said to Brother Blacksnake, "Brother Blacksnake, I know you said that you must be longer than this pole, but it's kind of cool this morning and you aren't stretching your length. Let me tie your one end and stretch you and I bet you would stretch much more than the pole."

20 Brother Rabbit took the head part of Brother Blacksnake, where the neck is, and tied it to the pole. Then he went to the tail part, stretched it, and tied it to the pole. Then he tied him in the middle part, put him on his shoulder, and took him to Father.

Brother Rabbit went back home. He took a gourd, cut off the end of the stem part and cleaned out all of the insides. Then he took a corn cob and put it in the opening, put it on his head, and walked until he came to a big old bee tree where there were plenty of bees.

de pole is.

Buh Rabbit tell Buh Black Sneak say, "Buh Black Sneak, uh know say yo mus' is long mo' en dis yuh pole, but e kine uh coolish dis mawnin en yo ain tretch yo lenk. Lemme tide yo on e en', en tretch yo, en uh bet yo would tretch tummuch mo' 'en da pole."

20 Buh Rabbit tek de head pa-a-t uh Buh Black Sneak whey e neck fuh dey, en e tide um tuh de pole. Den e gone tuh de tail pa-at en e tretch um en e tide um tuh de pole. Den e tide um duh middle pa-a-t en e put um on e shoulder en e tek um tuh Farrer.

Buh Rabbit gone back home en e tek on e goad en e cut out de en' uh de stem pa-a-t off clean en clean all de eenside out clean. En e tek one cawn cob en shet up de mout, en put um on e head en e walk tell e meet up wid one big ole bee tree whey nuf uh bee dey dey.

Buh Rabbit tell Buh Bee say, "Good mawnin, Buh Bee." Buh Bee tell um say, "Good mawnin, Buh Rabbit."

Buh Rabbit say, "Buh Bee, nuf uh younna dey een da tree, entty?"

Brother Rabbit said to Brother Bee, "Good morning, Brother Bee." Brother Bee said, "Good morning, Brother Rabbit."

Brother Rabbit said, "Brother Bee, you've got plenty of bees in the tree, don't you?"

Brother Bee told Brother Rabbit that the tree was so big that they hadn't had to swarm out of the tree in three years time.

25   Brother Rabbit said, "Great peace, Brother Bee, there's enough of you all in that tree that would almost fill up this gourd."

Brother Bee said to Brother Rabbit, "Get serious, man. Half of us couldn't fit in that gourd."

Brother Rabbit said, "I don't know, Brother Bee, this is one very big gourd. I bet every one of you all can't go in it. If only one of you is left out, you win."

Brother Rabbit set the gourd on the ground and he took out the corn cob that shut the mouth of the gourd, and the bees went into the gourd. Z-Z-Z-Z-Z-Z, until they all went into the gourd. When all had flown in, Brother Rabbit put the corn cob back in the mouth and he

Buh Bee tell Buh Rabbit say de tree so big tell e ain hads fuh swarm out de tree een tree ears time.

25   Buh Rabbit say, "Great peace, Buh Bee, nuf uh younna dey een da tree fuh mos' full up dis yuh goad."

Buh Bee tell Buh Rabbit say, "Gullong, man. Half uh we couldn' go een da goad."

Buh Rabbit say, "Uh dunno, Buh Bee, dis yuh duh one berry big goad. Uh bet ebby one uh younna can' go een um. Ef only tuh one uh younna done lef out younna win."

Buh Rabbit set de goad on de groun en e tek out de cawn cob wuh does shet de mout eh de goad, en Buh Bee come een de goad, Z-Z-Z-Z-Z-Z, tell all done gone een de goad. When all done gone een, Buh Rabbit put de cawn cob back een de mout en put de gaod on e head en tek um tuh Farrer.

Buh Rabbit gone back home gen en e git one smood boad en e tek um en e rub um en e greasy um, en e rub um en e greasy um, tell e git um dis es slick es e kin is.

30   Buh Rabbit put de boad on a

71

put the gourd on his head and took it to Father.

Brother Rabbit went back home again and got a smooth board. He rubbed and greased it, and rubbed and greased it, until he got it just as slick as his kind is.

30   Brother Rabbit put the board on his head and he carried it down near where Brother Alligator lived and he threw it across a little creek that was there. Then he took his little mincing walk across the board. He went to Brother Alligator's house and met Brother Alligator sitting on his porch.

Brother Rabbit said to Brother Alligator, "Good morning, Brother Alligator. How do you do? I haven't seen you in a long time."

Brother Alligator said to Brother Rabbit, "Good morning, Brother Rabbit. It truly has been a long time since I've seen you."

Brother Rabbit told Brother Alligator that it was truly a long time since he had seen him and he had to come visiting to see how all of them were getting along.

Brother Rabbit then turned around and said to Brother Alligator,

head en tote um down nigh'st whey B'Allegetter lib, en e trowed um crost one leetle crick wuh dey dey. Den e take e little pim-pim walk acrost de boad. E gone tuh B'Allegetter house en meet B'Allegetter duh set on e poach.

Buh Rabbit tell B'Allegetter say, "Good mawnin, B'Allegetter. How yo all do? Uh ain see yo long time."

B'Allegetter tell Buh Rabbit say, "Good mawnin, Buh Rabbit, e is bin long time sence uh see yo fuh true."

Buh Rabbit tell B'Allegetter say e is duh long time fuh true sence e done shum en e hads fuh come fuh shum fuh see how all dem duh gittin long.

Buh Rabbit den tun roun en e tell B'Allegetter say, "B'Allegetter, uh bin uh comin long dis now en uh meet one boad dey cross one leetle crick. Da ting duh de slickes ting uh ebber see, uh bet e ain duh nuttin scusin tuh me uh one bud wuh kin walk cross da boad en don' fall off."

35   B'Allegetter say, "Gullong, buh Rabbit, yo always got summuch

"Brother Alligator, I was coming along just now and I came upon a board that was across a little creek. The thing was the slickest thing I ever saw. I bet there is nothing except me and a bird that can walk across that board and not fall off."

35   Brother Alligator said, "Go on, Brother Rabbit, you've always got too much to say for yourself. Anybody could've walked across that board."

Brother Rabbit said, "All right, Brother Alligator. If you don't believe, come on down and see for yourself." So they went down to where the board was, and Brother Rabbit walked mincingly across it.

Brother Alligator put his front feet on the board as if he were going to cross. His feet slipped off and, to catch himself, Brother Alligator grabbed the board in his mouth. His tusks fastened into the board and jerked out of his mouth. Brother Alligator himself went SAPLASH in the creek.

Brother Rabbit took the board with the tusks in it and carried it to Father.

Father gave Brother Rabbit

fuh say fuh yo self. Anybody could uh walk cross da board."

Buh Rabbit say, "All right, B'Allegetter, ef you done beleebe come on down and see fuh yowe self." So dem gone down wey de boad dey, en Buh Rabbit tek a leeple pim-pim walk en gone cross de boad.

B'Allegetter put e front foots on de boad en mek fuh go cross. E foots slip off en, fuh ketch e self, B'Allegetter grab de boad een e mout. E tursh fasen een de boad en juk out e mout, en B'Allegetter self gone SAPLASH een de crick.

Buh Rabbit tek de boad wid de tursh een um en e tek um tuh Farrer.

Farrer gie Buh Rabbit one bi-i-g box en e tell um say, "Buh Rabbit, yo fuh open dis yuh box een de middle uh de bigges fiel yo kin fine, en yo fuh open um dis day duh brukkin een de mawnin."

40   Buh Rabbit put de box on e head en e tote um all night long.

Dis day duh brukkin een de mawnin Buh Rabbit knock two de boad off de box en time e know off de two baod, two big houn jump out a big box and said to him, "Brother Rabbit, you open this box in the biggest field you can find, and you open it just as day is breaking in the morning."

40   Brother Rabbit put the box on his head and he toted it all night long.

Just as day was breaking in the morning, Brother Rabbit knocked two of the boards off the top of the box. The same time he knocked off the two boards, two big hounds jumped out in his face.

Brother Rabbit ran. The hounds ran. Brother Rabbit ran. The hounds ran. Every now and then they'd catch up with Brother Rabbit and bite off a piece of his long tail, and Brother Rabbit would keep running. After a little while, they'd catch up again. They'd get another piece of tail. Brother Rabbit kept going farther.

At about midday, Brother Rabbit got to some brush. Every time he ran in, a hound ran him out. He went to another. The hounds ran him out. That's what started the saying, "It's not every piece of brush that can hold a rabbit."

By and by, Brother Rabbit

een e face.

Buh Rabbit run. De houn run. Buh Rabbit run, de houn run. Ebby now en den dey ketch up wid Buh Rabbit en bite off piece e long tail, en Buh Rabbit gone yonder. Turrecly e ketch um gen, e gite nedder piece e tail, Buh Rabbit gone yonder.

Bout middle day Buh Rabbit git tuh some bresh. Time e run een one de houn run um out. E gone een tarrer de houn run um out. Dat cause uh de sayin, "E ain ebby piece uh bresh kin hole rabbit."

Bumby Buh Rabbit come tuh one holler log en e gone een um, en de houn couldn' git een dey at um. But dem houn dey-dey duh gnaw en duh scratch en duh try fuh git Buh Rabbit all de Gawd-sen' day.

45   Buh Rabbit had uh been tote da box all night long en run all de mawnin, e hongry en e tusty en e skay tuh det en e duh trimble all ober.

Dem houn stid dey tell black da-a-k fo dem gone home.

When Buh Rabbit know say dem gone, e come out de log en gone home, en nex mawnin e gone came to a hollow log and went inside, and the hounds couldn't get at him. But the hounds gnawed and they scratched and they tried to get at Brother Rabbit all the God-sent day.

45   Brother Rabbit had been carrying the box all night long and had been running all morning. He was hungry and he was thirsty. He was scared to death and he was trembling all over.

Those hounds stayed there until the blackest part of the night before they went home.

When Brother Rabbit knew they were gone, he came out of the log, and the next morning he went to see Father.

After Brother Rabbit addressed him with the proper courtesy, Father asked him what he wanted.

50   Brother Rabbit said to Father, "Father, you told me that if I was to do like you told me to do, I'd get more knowledge. You gave me those two hounds and they nearly killed me, and they bit off my long tail."

Father said to Brother Rabbit, "Come here." Brother

duh Farrer.

At e done mek e mannus, Farrer ax um wuh e does wa'.

50   Buh Rabbit tell Farrer say, "Farrer, yo tell me say ef uh was tuh do lukka how yo tell me say fuh do uh'd uh git mo acknowledge. Yo gimme dem two houn en de ting like fuh kill me, en dey done bite off muh long tail."

Farrer tell Buh Rabbit say, "Come yuh." Buh Rabbit gone tur um en Farrer tek um en pull e yays, e pull e yays, en e pull e yays long luk uh jackass yays.

Farrer den tell Buh Rabbit say, "Buh Rabbit, yo done fool all dem tarrer creeter but yo ain bin satify. Yo had fuh come yuh fuh try fuh fool me. Uh done pull yo yays long like a jackass yays en dem houn done bite off yo long tail, en e ain a gwine grow again, en duh so yo duh gwine troo life, en yo done loss de sense yo had."

Entty duh so yo meet Buh Rabbit today? E got e long yays, en e leetle shawt tail, en e ain got uh bit uh sense. En e git all uh dat fuh e try fuh fool Farrer.

Rabbit went towards him and
Father took him and pulled his ears,
he pulled his ears, and he pulled his
ears long like a jackass' ears.

The Father said to Brother
Rabbit, "Brother Rabbit, you fooled
all of those other creatures but you
weren't satisfied. You had to come
here and try to fool me. I have
pulled your ears long like a jackass'
ears and those hounds bit off your
long tail and it won't grow again,
and that's how you will go through
life. You have lost the sense you
once had."

Isn't that so when you meet
Brother Rabbit today? He has long
ears and a little short tail and he
doesn't have a bit of sense. He got
all of that because he tried to fool
Father.

46-B6

BROTHER RABBIT LOSES HIS HEAD

1   Brother Rabbit wouldn't let his wife leave the house at all. He said the house is the place where women stay. However, Brother Partridge let his wife go whenever she wanted to go.

Sister Partridge went to Brother Rabbit's house one time and asked Sister Rabbit to go down the road a bit with her. Sister Rabbit told her she couldn't go because Brother Rabbit didn't let her leave the house.

Sister Partridge went on, and when she got home she talked to Brother Partridge about it. Brother Partridge said he was going to make Brother Rabbit ashamed of himself for not letting his wife ever leave the house.

The next time he met up

46-B6

BUH RABBIT LOSES E HEAD

1   Buh Rabbit ain le' e wife go fuhm de house none tall. E tell um say house duh de place fuh oomans stay. Odderwise, Buh Pa'tridge does le' he wife go whey'd sonebber e does wa'n go.

Suh Pa'tridge gone tuh Buh Rabbit house one time en ax Suh Rabbit fuh go down de road uh piece wid um. Suh Rabbit tell um say e couldn' go cay Buh Rabbit don' does le' um go fuhm de house.

Suh Pa'tridge gone on, en when e gone home e talk tuh Buh Pa'tridge bout dat. Buh Pa'tridge say e duh gwine mek Buh Rabbit shame e self fo don't let e wife lef de house none tall.

Nex time e meet up wid Buh Rabbit, Buh Pa'tridge say, "Buh Rabbit, mek don' le' you wife come

with Brother Rabbit, Brother
Partridge said, "Brother Rabbit,
why don't you let your wife come
over to my house and see my old
woman?"

5   Brother Rabbit said, "I don't
let her leave the house at all. She
has to stay there all of the time."

Then Brother Partridge
asked Brother Rabbit what he left
with his wife to look at when she
was there all by herself.

Brother Rabbit told him
that he didn't leave anything there
for her to look at.

Brother Rabbit then asked
Brother Partridge what he left for
his wife to look at.

Brother Partridge said to
Brother Rabbit, "If I'm going to be
away from the house for a long
time, I leave my head for her to
look at. Then when I get back she
has combed my hair well and picked
everything out of it and has greased
it to make it look pretty. Then
when I get back, I put my head back
on and I'm ready to go anywhere."

10   Brother Rabbit told Brother
Partridge that he couldn't take his
head off.

ober tuh my house en see muh ole
ooman?"

5   Buh Rabbit say, "Uh don'
does le 'um lef de house none tall, e
haf fuh stey dey all de time."

Buh Pa'tridge den ax Buh
Rabbit wuh e does lef wid e wife fuh
look at when e dey dey by e'self.

Buh Rabbit tell um say e don'
does lef nuttin dey fuh e look at.

Buh Rabbit den ax Buh
Pa'tridge wuh him does lef fuh he
wife fuh look at.

Buh Pa'tridge tell Buh
Rabbit say, "Ef uh duh gwine fuh be
off fuhm de house long time, uh
does lef muh head fuh e look at.
Den when uh git back e ha' comb
muh hay good, en pick all de oul en
ting out, en has done greasy um en
mek um look pooty, den when uh
come back e does put muh head
back on puntop me, en uh ready
fuh go ennwhey."

10   Buh Rabbit tell Buh
Pa'tridge say e can' does tek e head
off.

Buh Pa'tridge tell Buh
Rabbit say, "Uh duh gwine home
right now en uh does gwine lef muh

Brother Partridge said to Brother Rabbit, "I'm going home right now and I'm going to leave my head. Wait here till I come back. I'll show you I can do it."

Brother Rabbit waited there, and soon Brother Partridge came back with his head underneath his wing. Brother Rabbit saw it looked like he didn't have a head and he asked him, "Brother Partridge, how are you able to walk about if you don't have a head?"

Brother Partridge said to Brother Rabbit, "Didn't I tell you I was going home to leave my head?"

Then Brother Rabbit asked Brother Partridge, "How can you talk without a head? Where is your mouth?"

15   Brother Partridge then told Brother Rabbit that he didn't have to have a head to talk. He can talk and he can see all around without his head.

Brother Rabbit was completely taken in. He went home and said to his old woman, "I'm going to leave something nice to keep you company when I'm away from you."

head. Wait yuh tell uh come back, uh'l show you uh kin do um."

Buh Rabbit waid dey en turrecly Buh Pa'tridge come back wid e head on'neet e wing. Buh Rabbit shum look luk e ain gots no head en e ax um, "Buh Pa'tridge, huccome you able fuh walk bout en ain gots no head?"

Buh Pa'tridge tell Buh Rabbit say, "Entty uh tell you say uh duh gwine home fuh lef muh head?"

Buh Rabbit den ax Buh Pa'tridge, "How you fuh talk en ain gots no head? Whey you mout dey?"

15   Buh Pa'tridge den tell Buh Rabbit e ain haffuh ha head fuh talk, e kin talk en e kin see fuh go all erbout bidout e head.

Buh Rabbit bin all tek up wid dat, en e gone home en tell e ole ooman say, "Uh duh gwine lef suppin nice fuh keep you comp'ny when uh does be gone fuhm yuh."

De ooman ax um wuh duh him e duh gwine lef. Buh Rabbit tell um say him gwine lef muh head.

De ooman tell um say e ain

The woman asked him what he was going to leave. Brother Rabbit told her that he was going to leave his head.

The woman told him that he couldn't leave his head.

Brother Rabbit always wanted to act important and he said to the woman, "Yes, I can leave my head. When I leave, it will be company for you to talk to."

20   The woman told him again he couldn't leave his head, but Brother Rabbit was so arrogant, he thought he could do anything Brother Partridge could do. He said to the woman, "Come here. I'll show you how I can leave my head for you."

Brother Rabbit got the axe and he laid his head on the chopping block. He told his wife to take the axe and cut his head off. The woman told him that she wasn't going cut his head off because it would kill him. Brother Rabbit assured her, "It isn't going to kill me. All you have to do when I come back is put my head on again."

The woman told him again she wasn't going to cut his head off,

kin lef e head, Buh Rabbit does always wan' ack biggity, en e tell de ooman say, "Yeh uh is kin lef muh head, en when uh done lef um ee'l be comp'ny fuh you fuh talk tuh you."

20   De ooman tell um gen say e couldn' lef e head, but Buh Rabbit so biggety tell e does tink him kin do enny ting Buh Pa'tridge kin do, en e tell do ooman say, "Come yuh, uhl show you how uh kin lef muh head fuh yuh."

Buh Rabbit gone git de ax en gone lay e head on de choppin block en e tell e wife fuh tek de ax en cut e head off. De ooman tell um say e ain duh gwine cut e head off fuh kill um. Buh Rabbit say, "E ain duh gwine kill me. All you haf fuh do when uh come back, put muh head on gen."

De ooman tell um gen say e ain duh gwine cut e head off, but Buh Rabbit quarl wid de ooman summuch tell e git kine ub uh bex wid Buh Rabbit, en e tell um say, "Ef you wan' you head cut off, uh'l cut um off, but duh you mek me do um." So de ooman tek de ax en come down, BAM, puntop Buh Rabbit neck en pa't e head fuhm e body.

but Brother Rabbit quarreled with the woman so much that she got angry with Brother Rabbit. She said to him, "If you want your head cut off, I'll cut it off, but you made me do it." So the woman took the axe and came down, BAM! upon Brother Rabbit's neck, and parted his head from his body.

Instead of Brother Rabbit getting up and walking off, he just kicked his leg, bliff bliff bliff bliff, stiffened out, and died right there.

When the woman saw that Brother Rabbit was dead for sure, she ran to Brother Partridge's house and told him what had happened.

25   Brother Partridge told the woman it wasn't her fault; it was all because Brother Rabbit acted so self-important.

They all had a big wake that night, and the next day all of the creatures on Daufuskie Island went to the funeral.

'Stid uh Buh Rabbit git up e walk off e dis kick e laig, bliff, bliff, bliff, bliff, en stiffen out en dead right dey.

When de ooman see Buh Rabbit done dead fuh true, e run gone tuh Buh Pa'tridge house en tell um huccome e tuh happen.

25   Buh Pa'tridge tell de ooman say ain duh um fault, but e all fuh Buh Rabbit fuh wa' ack so biggety.

Dem all had uh big setting up da night, en nex day all uh dem gone tuh de funedrul.

TRANSLATOR'S NOTE

My translation of these stories does not adhere to any academic protocol or standard. My purpose was the popularization of the literature found in the Gullah language.

Though I am not uncomfortable with balancing precariously on a branch of academia, attempting to define the language of my translation as "Contemporary English" borders on the ridiculous. The paradigm dialect (of what might more properly be defined as "Conversational America") that I have tried to follow could be described as "Mid-Atlantic Suburban American." This is the dialect that predominates the linguistic geography from Chester County, Pennsylvania, to Indianapolis, including portions of New York State and the southern tier of Connecticut. Accessibility being my primary motivation, the manner of speech I have tried to use might be called "Ohioid."

In my translation, I have followed the paragraph separations of Mr. Stoddard's Gullah transliteration of his Library of Congress recordings. Each paragraph of Stoddard's Gullah text, thus, corresponds to each paragraph of the translation. Hopefully, this will prevent any overly liberal translations of which I might be guilty from compounding the reader's confusing for more than one paragraph within the course of a particular story.

Against the protests of my august and intrepid associate editor, Lewis Hammet, I have chosen not to "correct" or revise the punctuation found in Mr. Stoddard's original typescript, although it does not conform to MLA standards. Without the benefit of consultation with Mr. Stoddard himself, I am opposed to second-guessing his reasoning for the insertion or deletion of the pauses implied by comma or period placement. I suspect that cadence or the rhythmic pronunciations of sentence structure (*see introduction*) may point to nuances of meaning in the West African Gullah language. Thus, except for a few possible typographical errors, I leave it for later interpreters to alter.

GULLAH GLOSSARY

Able – big
Acknowledge – knowledge
Aig – edge, egg
Akon – acorn
At – after
Ax – ask(ed)
Baig – beg
Bayfoot – barefoot
Beer – bear
Bex – vex(ed)
Beyobs – herbs
Bidout – without
Biggety – indignant, proud
Bittle – victual (food)
Bleebe – believe
Boad – board
Breeze – breathe
Bresh – brush, undergrowth
Bret – breath
Brukkin – daybreak
Bud – bird
Buh – brother
Bum, bumby – by and by, after a while
Bun – burn
B'Olifaum – Brother Elephant
Cay – because
Cayjon – occasion
Cha-a-am – charm
Chook – put
Chune – tune
Compersation – conversation
Cooter – terrapin
Creeter – creature(s)
Curtschey – curtsy
Day clean – sun above the horizon; daybreak
Dey-dey, deydey – there are, there

Diddy – here
Dis – just as
Dizac – exact
Dreen – drain
Duh – the, who was, that
Dunk'yer – did not care
E – he, she, his, her, it
E self – himself, herself
Ear – air
Ears – years
Een – in, into, end
En, ent – is not
Entty – isn't it so
Exwansus – advantage (of)
Farrer – Father, God
Fench – fence
Figger – figure(s), as in the patters represented in certain group dances
Fuh – for, in order to
Fuh whuf fuh – why
Gawd – God
Gen – against, again
Goad – gourd
Greyshish – gracious
Gwine – going, going to, preparing to
Habes – harvest
Hay – hair
Him – him, he, her, she
Hi' – hoist
Hut – hurt
Jew – dew
Jook – joke, fool
Juk – jerk
Kin – can, able to
Laig – leg, legged
Leases – smallest
Leddown – lie down, lay down

Leek – lick
Lif – edge, lip
Lukka – like, same as
Ma-a-sh – marsh
Ma'kin – markings, characteristics
Mannus – manners
Ma'sheen – Marsh Hen
Medjur – measure
Meet – found, came upon, discovered
Mek – why, make
Mine – tend to
Minimit – minute
Nedder – more, another
Niece – regardless of gender, one's
    brother or sister's children
Nummer – except
Nuse – use
Nyam, n'yam – chew
Nyung – young
Oasmen – oarsmen
Olifaum – elephant
On'neet – underneath, beneath
Ooman – woman
P'yon – pure
Pa-a-t – part
Panch – pant
Pick e box – play guitar, banjo, etc.
Pledger – pleasure
Pooty – pretty
Pos' – post
Projec – prowling or crusing; light-
    hearted, often mischievous wandering
Puntop – on, upon, on top of, at
Putter – potato
Qua'il – quarrel
Quile – coil
Res – rest
S' – sister or Mrs.
Sage – sedge grass

Scusin – except, let alone
Shay – share
Sho – shore
Shum – saw it, saw him
Skayed – scared
Sneak – snake
Stan – look(s)
Stid – stayed
'Stid – instead
Study – think, thought, reflect upon
Suh – sister
Sukka – such as, like
Tall – at all
Tarrer – other
Taught – thought
Tay – tear
Tek tarrer – the other
Tell – until
Tide – tie
Tim-pim – mincing, exceptionally proper
Tippity – antipathy
Trimble – tremble
Troo – through
Tummuch – very much
Tun – turn
Tursh – tusk
Tusty – thirsty
Uh – I
Wey – where
Wul – world
Wut – worth anything (worthless)
Yays – ears
Yeddy – hear, listen, heard
Yent – could not
Yie – eye
Younna – like you
Yuh – here
Yuhin – hearing
Yut – earth

BIBLIOGRAPHY

Burn, Billie. *An Island Named Daufuskie*. Spartanburg: The
  Reprint Company, 1991.

Gleason, Judith Illsley. *Orisha: The Gods of Yorubaland*. New York:
  Antheneum, 1971.

Gonzales, Ambrose E. *The Black Border*. Spartanburg: The
  Reprint Company, 1991.

Jaquith, Priscilla, ed. *Bo Rabbit Smart for True: Tall Tales of
  the Gullah*. New York: Putnam, 1994.

Jones-Jackson, Patricia. *When Roots Die*. Athens: Brown
  Thrasher Books, 1987.

Miller, Edward. *Gullah Statesman: Robert Smalls, from
  Slavery to Congress, 1839-1915*. Columbia: U of
  South Carolina P, 1994.

Montgomery, Michael. *Crucible of Carolina: Essays on the
  Development of Gullah Language & Culture*. Athens:
  U of Georgia P, 1994.

Turner, Lorenzo. *Africanisms in the Gullah Dialect*. New
  York: Ayer Company, 1969.

CREDITS

Albert H. Stoddard:	Storyteller (transcription)
Will Killhour:	Senior Editor (selection, sequence, translation, editing)
Ruth Gaul Killhour:	Consulting Editor
Lewis Hammet:	Associate Editor (typography, copy editing, layout)
Christina Bates:	Illustrator
Karen Burlingame:	Data Coordinator
Lori Soergel:	Administrative Assistant
Wellesley Greenwood:	Managing Editor
Bookcrafters:	Printing & Binding
Pubert:	Cat-Under-Foot

89